RANEAN
ENTURY B.C

YRIA

Sea

Cannae

Euxine Sea

MACEDONIA

BITHYNIA

Tarentum

Thurii

Cynoscephalae

Aegean
Sea

Pergamum

ASIA

Magnesia

Crotona

Ephesus

CAPPADOCIA

Athens

Antioch

use

Rhodes

Ionian Sea

Cyprus

PHOENICIA

Crete

Tyre

Cyrene

Barca

EGYPT

R. Nile

CARTHAGE

CARTHAGE

A NOVEL BY
ROSS LECKIE

CANONGATE

First published in Great Britain in 2000 by Canongate Books
14 High Street, Edinburgh EH1 1TE, Scotland

Published simultaneously in the United States
of America and Canada in 2001 by
Canongate Books Ltd

10 9 8 7 6 5 4 3 2

British Library Cataloguing-in-Publication Data
A catalogue record for this book is available on
request from the British Library

ISBN 0 86241 944 1

Typeset by Palimpsest Book Production Limited,
Polmont, Stirlingshire

Printed and bound by
Creative Print and Design, Ebbw Vale, Wales

Conticuere omnes intentique ora tenebant.
inde toro pater Aeneas sic orsus ab alto:
infandum, regina, iubes renovare dolorem,
Troianas ut opes et lamentabile regnum
eruerint Danai, quaeque ipse miserrima Uidi
et quorum pars magna fui. quis talia fando
Myrmidonum Dolopumve aut duri miles ulixi
temperet a lacrimis? et iam nox umida caelo
praecipitat suadentque cadentia sidera somnos.
sed si tantus amor casus cognoscere nostros
et breviter Troiae supremum audire laborem,
quamquam animus meminisse horret luctuque refugit,
incipiam.

They all fell silent, each face turned intently towards him. Then from his couch high up, father Aeneas began: 'You bid me, O queen, revive an unutterable sorrow; how the Greeks erased Troy and its magnificence, ever worth mourning. I saw that tragedy myself, indeed I was at its core. No one, not even a Myrmidon or a Dolopian, not even some soldier of unpitying Ulysses could tell this tale and fail to weep. Well, the damp air of night is falling swiftly from the sky. The setting stars remind us that we too must sleep. But if you really want to learn what befell us and to hear the gist of Troy's last trial, even though I shrink from the memory and can barely face its pain, yet I will begin.'

VIRGIL, *Aeneid* II, 1–13

Contents

Prologue

I am Polybius, a prince, a Greek, but I write this in Rome. We came back here from Carthage, and destruction. Scipio, whom I serve, still wakes at night, sweating, screaming at the memory of what we have seen – and been. Not even in Sofonisa, his wife, can he find the succour that he seeks.

What we have been? I should say 'he'. It was Scipio who allowed Cato to force him to war, to lead the Roman army, to root out Carthage like an old olive tree in the way of a new road. Now Scipio cannot bear what he has done.

Such is the way of history, implacable as night and ineluctable. I should know, for though born to high estate I am now an historian and scholar, writing the history of Rome's rise, of Carthage's fall in the same year as Rome also destroyed the once great Greek city of Corinth.

I fought the Romans once. It no longer seems a prudent thing to do. We Greeks lost at the battle of Pydna, twenty-two years ago, and I was brought, a hostage, in chains to Rome. After years of misery, Scipio rescued me. I had been working as a clerk and translator in the archives of the Senate, a slave of inventories, depositions, deeds. But Scipio saw my promise. I—. Enough of me. I do not need to record that. My works will be sufficient for memorial.

I was present at Carthage's final fall. Scipio had me search the city's citadel for papers, and in particular for anything that might confirm the duplicity of Cato. What if anything that will achieve, if proved, I do not know.

I found a great deal. Hanno, it seemed, had ordered much of Carthage's archive moved to the citadel for safety. What I found germane in that is here. But what I read led me to seek out more, not only here in Rome but also in Capua, Neapolis and elsewhere.

Romans love their records. Theirs is a race that needs to feel secure. It is a custom of this people that on his death all a man's extant correspondence must be lodged, in the appropriate office, with his will. So I have had many archives on which to draw, all catalogued and sound.

And, thanks to Scipio, I have had unimpeded access to the records of the Republic, the speeches of the Senate, all of Cato's papers and even what used to be his room in the Curia. It has been preserved as what I can only call a shrine. There are still boxes of unread papers there.

This book is the result of my researches. Here, principally, is Hanno, the bastard son of the great general Hannibal who so nearly destroyed Rome. Here too is the man who once was mapmaker to Hannibal, then secretary to Scipio Africanus and finally guardian of Hanno. Bostar of Chalcedon's life is a strange one, even in the myriad ways of men.

His journal was written in rather elegant Greek. I hope to have done it justice, but then Latin is not an easy language into which to translate Greek. It lacks the elasticity, the fecundity of the queen of tongues. Hanno's memoir he wrote in Punic, the language of the Carthaginians. It is inflected and testing, but fortunately a language I have known all my life. From its foundation, my home city of Megalopolis in Arcadia plied rich trade with Carthage. My nurse, Salambo, was Carthaginian, and I learned Punic first from her.

For Rome, albeit in the shadows here is Scipio, son of the great Scipio Africanus who saved Rome but could not save himself – I should add bastard son, for the Scipio I serve is as Hanno was: two bastards doomed in life to seek each other's death. Who needs the fictions of the poets when we have such facts as these?

Here also is Cato, self-made man, senator and later Censor and, for reasons apparent or not from what follows (that judgement being yours), opponent with his every breath of the Scipios – and Carthage.

I have added the occasional note of explanation or exegesis, and there are many other voices here. The selection is mine, idiosyncratic, and seeks only to replicate life. 'πολλὰ τὰ δεινὰ κοὐδὲν ἀνθρώπου δεινότερον πέλει' – 'Strange wonders are many,' says Sophocles in his play Antigone, 'but none is stranger than man.' So what follows is not history. That is the study of forces which shape the world, for all man's attempts to hew it other ways.

The formal history I am writing tells that Carthage fell. Let this book, its ghosts and dreams and voices, tell how and why. Let it be a companion to my history, and even bring to historiography something new: 'pragmatic history', involving the study of contemporary documents and memoirs, we might call it.

But if the questions of how and why are simple, the answers are complex. That is because they lie of course in people: in their aspirations; fears and fickle foibles; fatal flaws; in, above all, the ambiguity of action. As I believe this work shows, it is by a series of mistakes that some states thrive and others fall. There is no visionary's plan. There are only the disasters some people spawn, though why we cannot tell, and others' dreams. States emerge from in between, and Rome is not expanding. It is realising. It is an inalienable fact of history that some get in her way.

So, a medley, a mosaic; tesserae would be the Latin word for what is here. It is a story that has entered now the labile mists of memory. As Aristotle urges us of drama, 'suspend your disbelief.' Expect no consistency, no disciplined chronology here. Most of these lives are ended. Only marks on wax or parchment prove that they have ever been.

From Hanno's memoir, found among his papers in the citadel of Carthage

We are surrounded now. They have broken through the walls, and possess the city, bar this citadel where I am; I, Hanno, son of a legend and a slave; Bostar, bent with years, who has been my guardian, mentor and friend, father I never had; Fetopa, my wife, whom I have learned to love in as many ways as rain comes.

Here with me also are our four children Fetopa holds as a hen does her chicks against the deepening of the dark; Artixes, a doctor and man learned in many things; Halax, rich in the lore of plants and animals, a hunchback but my friend; Tancinus, once a Roman, now no man; some hundred of my people who have come with me to the farthest reach of hope and of endurance. And I have the sacred books, the soul of Carthage.

High on the sacred mountain Jebel-bou-Kournine, still our beacon burns. I will see its light tonight, and our strength will be renewed. We will mock the Romans. The walls girding us are thick and strong, built, our legends tell us, not by any man but by Tanit-pene-Baal, great goddess of the moon and of forgetfulness. We have time, water, food. None of the Romans, not even Scipio, whoever helps him, can know of all our secret stores and cisterns, deep hewn from rock when Rome was only huddled huts, squatting by the Tiber. So let them seek the ruins' shelter from this summer sun that beats and pounds and sears the brain.

I can see the sea from here, hear the water's sounding, ceaseless sibilance. And from the sea, help may come before I do that which otherwise will be done. The wood is seasoned, dry. The pyre stands by. Meanwhile, let me write – and others too – of how it came to be that, once again, Rome confronted Carthage.

I begin that which now is almost ended. I go back, back. To Macedonia, and to a boy waiting, waiting for his father, Hannibal. Yes, let that be where I begin. I shut my eyes against my people's noise. Blind, I see. Eyes open again, sweat plopping off my forehead from the heat, the stench of many people and no wind, eyes only on the vellum here before me and the goose-quill's point, I write.

Letter from Cato's papers, preserved in the archives
of Rome

To Marcus Porcius Cato, Censor, in Rome; Quintus Vitellius Tancinus, special legate, sends greetings from Sicily. I have followed your orders to the letter. Leaving Rome, and satisfied that no persons matching your description of them had sailed from Ostia, I enquired at all the harbours of the south-western littoral: Misenum, Neapolis, Posidonia, Elea and Rhegium. I could find no trace of them. So I assumed that this Bostar and the bastard Hanno had not, as you feared, gone south to Carthage.

Still, I crossed to Sicily and, using your warrant and your gold, asked at Panormus and Messana. Nothing. At Agrigentum and Gela. Nothing. Only in Syracuse did I find good – and expensive – news. A galley called the *Apollodorus*, double-oared and fast, its master one Trimalchio, a Ligurian. This Bostar chartered her some five months ago. Trimalchio did not leave an itinerary with the harbourmaster as he should have done. But all my sources are agreed: the *Apollodorus* sailed east, with enough provisions for a long journey. I questioned the port's quartermaster. He remembered the transaction clearly. Among other strange things, this Bostar insisted on a large package of that strange gum, *bdellium*. Where have they gone? To Achaea, Epirus or Macedonia? Asia, Lycia or even Bithynia where, they say, that savage Hannibal hides? If you want me to search in the east, I suggest I take ship to Athens. You say this Bostar is a philhellene. Wherever he has gone he will have wanted, I believe, to refill the ship's water barrels there. I await your orders. By the hand of him who bears this, send them to me at the house of Pollius by the harbour wall – and send me more gold.

From Hanno's memoir

On the eastern edges of the sea I saw a sudden ship's sails shimmer in the dying of the light. Sitting at my supper on the terrace of our villa, I knew that it was him. I dropped my spoon, wrenched back my chair. I must have knocked over a cup. I heard the tinkle of its breaking on the mosaic of the floor. Ignoring Arxes' cries of protest, heart pounding, mind racing, I ran across the hall, out of the door, slipping, skidding on the road's mossed stones, bursting towards the little harbour and the shore.

There was nothing there. From where I had stopped, the pier's legs reached into dark. Hurrying home, three pigeons crossed the sky above me. Out to sea, a gull sped along the undulating, listless waves and gave its ululating call. A eulogy, an elegy, I do not know. I never have liked gulls. Sailors say they are departed souls.

Wind stirred the hillside's trees and they whispered to themselves like lovers, lost in what they believe. On the susurrating shingle, with a sudden shiver against the cooling air of evening, I sat down. My father, my father. I had waited already for so long.

First faint, then full: 'Boom, boom!' sounded through the silence. I looked up. No wind at all, a barely heaving sea. A drum. The steady drum for rowers' strokes. Of course, the wind had failed. That is why he had been so long. It was almost dark. The western sky still held low, palisading light. Then I heard the plashing, sucking, creaking of the oars. 'Hanno!' 'Hann-o!' I heard our servant Arxes' plaintive voice far behind me, up the hill. Looking back, I saw his lamp. I stood up. Carefully, because the pier's planks were cracked and sere, I made my way along.

I sensed the ship's shape before I saw it, massing in the dark. 'Deck one, ship oars!' came the mate's cry. 'Deck two!' Gliding silently, the galley was almost alongside. I waved with both arms. 'Father!' I shouted, 'Fath-er!' And then, in one light leap a man was on the pier beside me, holding me in his arms and, if he could have seen them, there were tears in my eyes.

But his was a smell I knew. My head muffled in his shoulder, I came to understand, wanted to shout 'No! No!' But with anger, I felt hope. I couldn't breathe. My hands on the man's shoulders, I pushed myself away and, in the light of a row of torches now burning along the galley's thwarts, looked up to see the face. It was not of the man I had dreamed and hoped for. But it was that of my, and my father's, dearest friend.

'Bostar? Bostar?' I whispered.

I saw it in his eyes, those deep, dark pools that had followed my father into the Alps and had already seen my half-brother die and, and – His face was set. His eyes were grave. His mouth was pinched. He opened it to speak.

'Your bags, Bostar of Chalcedon?' From our voyage to Macedonia I recognised the voice of Trimalchio, the shipmaster.

Still with his arms around me, 'What do you think, you fool!' Bostar snapped.

I started. I had never heard him speak like that before.

'Have them taken to the house, Trimalchio,' he went on. 'And see me in the morning.' There was a weariness, a sadness in his voice. It comes, I know now, of suffering.

Bostar turned towards the shore. 'Come, Hanno,' he said quietly.

'But my father, Bostar? My father?'

'Not now, Hanno, not now. Come.'

I thought then he was cruel. Now I think otherwise.

I saw Arxes' lamp come bobbing towards the pier. I followed Bostar, the porter and Arxes home. Perhaps it was clouds, or wind, or some far-off squall of rain. But as I walked back, I swear by Moloch, in the spreading sky above me I saw the stars set, one by fading one.

That was many years ago. I was a boy. Now I am a man, and so must leave the things of a child. I have known the joy of loving, and have not been afraid. Is that because I have known also the paths of pain?

Bostar declined Arxes' offer of a bath and, with barely a nod to me, went straight to his room bearing, it seemed, the weight of wordless fears. Arxes asked me if I wanted to finish my supper. I said no. He grunted, and I also went to my room. I did not sleep. I heard the barking of the dog fox, the bullfrog, the cricket and the hooting of the owl. I thought of my mother Apurnia, of my childhood in Capua, of how a strange, dark man came and took me from there. Of what he had told me, and taught me, of how he had tried. I dozed. I dreamed of falling, falling, and of being rescued by a huge white swan. I woke, sweating, to a sullen dawn and the smell of cookfires rising from the beach.

I asked Bostar over breakfast. He shook his head. 'Eat first,' he said. There were dark hollows above his cheekbones, and new lines crinkling the skin around his eyes.

'I'm not hungry.'

'Eat.' I did as I was told.

Arxes cleared the plates. Bostar fixed his great, luminous eyes on me, his pupils black, his irises white but raced with red. I noticed how his beard was streaked with new grey. He drew a deep breath, exhaled and, back straight, put his hands out flat on the table in front of him. I heard Arxes close the kitchen door.

'Hanno,' he said quietly but distinctly, his voice neutral, measured. 'Your father Hannibal is dead.'

What did I feel? I can't remember. 'H-ow?' I managed. Bostar closed his eyes, and continued in a monotone.

'Naked, alone in a room in the palace of Prusias in Sinope, he took his own life, rather than submit to Rome.'

A breeze teased through the open window. In the kitchen, Arxes clanked and swore. I hid my face in my hands, but I had to know more, more.

'Poison?' I asked, looking up, straining forward. I remember tripping on the Latin word *venenum*. We used to speak in Latin then, the language in which I was reared. Thanks to Bostar, I came to know several languages. I know more now, but do not know which is my own. Punic, I suppose. The language of my wife and people, the language of my dreams.

'No, not poison. He used, he used—' Bostar reached into the pocket of his tunic – 'this.' Onto the table of polished oak, he put a dagger, sheathed. Its handle was of some wood blacker than I had ever seen before. It lay between us, a threat, an accusation.

'Where—' I cleared my throat. 'Where did you get this, Bostar?'

'I bought it. In Bithynia, where as you know your father took refuge, or so he thought, everything can be bought. Including a man's life.'

'You mean my father was betrayed by King Prusias?'

'Betrayed? I don't know. The whole world now kneels to the Romans. They sent a message to Prusias, full of the usual felicities. But its meaning was clear: a cohort was coming to arrest your father. Prusias could let them, or stop them and wait for a legion, then more.'

'So he handed my father over?'

'No. He told him the Romans were coming; offered him the chance to escape. "I am now a bird grown too old to fly," your father replied. Or so it is said. The Romans found him waiting, but they were too late.'

My tears came fast and hot and stinging, from a part of me I had not known was there. Bostar got up, crossed the room and, standing behind me, put his hands on my shoulders, and ran them through my hair.

'Yes, cry, Hanno. Our tears will be your father's only funeral.'

I turned round. He was crying too. I stumbled up, into his arms. My sobs stilled. My anger grew. 'What, Bostar, what,' I mumbled into his woollen tunic, 'did they do with the body?'

Bostar stiffened, let go of me and rubbed his eyes with the heels of his hands. 'Come out onto the terrace, Hanno. I want to see the light.' Overlooking the pellucid pallor of the Aegean, his back to me, he went on.

'We will talk of your father's death only this once, Hanno. Then we will turn to your life, and his through yours. But you are his son, and only living legacy. You have a right to know.'

Bostar's knuckles whitened as he gripped the terrace rail, and his voice was tight and strained. 'The Romans had your father's body thrown into the city's cesspit. I was— I was two days late. When I left your father's service those years ago as he returned to Carthage, I did not want to save him. When I went to Bithynia, my mind had changed. Too late, too late.'

'But they didn't, didn't—'

'Didn't what?'

'Mutilate the body in any way?'

'No.'

'How can you be so sure?'

'Because I talked at length to the slaves who carried the corpse. They respected your father, or at least feared him. In Bithynia, as right across the world, he had become a name. Anyway, one of them, his name was Sottos, then cleaned your father's room. It was from Sottos I bought the dagger on the table there. Now it's yours.'

'So that is all I have of my father?'

'No, Hanno. No,' Bostar replied patiently, gently, turning round to look at me. 'You have his blood. You bear his name – and fame.'

Despatch in the hand of Speusippus, secretary to Cato the Censor, preserved in the archives of Rome

Marcus Porcius Cato the Censor to Lucius Antonius Regulus, Admiral of the Eastern Fleet. More and more breaches of our maritime laws are coming to my attention. Not all cargoes and itineraries are being registered. In particular, I have information about a double-oared galley called the *Apollodorus*, its master one Trimalchio, a Ligurian. In violation of the regulations it left Syracuse without declaring its destination, and is now thought to be in the east. Tell your ships, and those of our allies. The *Apollodorus* is to be seized on sight, its cargo confiscated, and its master and any passengers brought under guard to me here in Rome. If they resist arrest, they are to be killed. This is a matter vital to the welfare of the Republic. I see from this week's gazette that your nephew Falco is seeking an aedileship. I am sure you will not disappoint me.

Letter found among the papers of Titus Licinius
Labienus, magistrate in Capua, and preserved in the
consistory of the Capuan courts

My dear friend. If the seal is broken, read no more but burn this at once. Even under torture you cannot disclose what you do not know.

You will I am sure like all the world have heard the news by now. I reached Sinope only to find Hannibal dead, by his own hand. We had a hard voyage of it, against contrary winds but that does not matter now. I found no evidence that King Prusias or any others were involved. There is a limit, it seems, to the length of even Cato's arms. I think that Hannibal had just come to his end. We grieve for him with heavy hearts. Yet he will not wholly die. I wish him speed across the river of Forgetfulness, Ashroket in his Punic tongue, and pray he may be free. As he would have wished, I go on, and hope that mourning turns to morning.

I have been back here in Macedonia for three days. Hanno has taken the news very badly. He can think only of revenge. A loss, an anger burns in him that I can only watch and leave to run its course – although I am treating him with nepenthe and a little narceine. Tell Artixes. I think he would approve. But I have a plan in hand, of which I will tell Hanno when it is time. Although Trimalchio says otherwise, I do not trust the messenger to whom I am about to give this – a surly Illyrian sailor, with a poxed face and one eye. So I will not disclose to you now where I have decided we should go. I will write to you again when we get there – assuming we find ourselves among friends.

Meanwhile, I ask you now to proceed at once with the task I set you. It is vital that you find – *[Here the parchment was faded and cracked.]* . . . Hispala . . . name . . . north. Ask . . .tus Curtius . . . help. Silve. . . bankers . . . Massilia, by the west gate. Only way . . . avoid . . . war.

Give Artixes my greetings. Tell Apurnia her son Hanno is, under the circumstances, well.

From Hanno's memoir

The characters were strange. Bostar had started teaching me spoken Punic as soon as we left Capua. And an old Carthaginian merchant from the nearby town of Amphipolis came each day for conversation while Bostar was away. Then I began to learn the writing. Punic was my father's language, of course, although he spoke many more. Greek was his polyglot army's language of command, but I know from Bostar how he could even talk to the Gauls in their own guttural tongue. Anyway, I studied Punic to help take away the pain. Bostar spent most of each day in his room writing letters. Two or three messengers came and went most days, and the captain Trimalchio was often with us too, shut up with Bostar in his room. I remember thinking I might write to my mother in my new-found Punic. But then I realised. She would not understand.

Letter found among Cato's papers and preserved in the archives of Rome. The hand was crude, the grammar poor and the Latin strange. But it is reproduced here as faithfully as my papyrology allows

My wife. I hope this will finds you well, if as is it finds you at all which I am not sure of. The wind has been from the north now these past days, and seeing as you know that do not agree with my bones. The word is how the Eastern Fleet has stepped up its patrols. No one knows why. They are searching every ship, they say, and intercepting mail. It's like when that devil Hannibal was loose, but I'm sure as they will have done for him by now. For me, I am earning a living as best as what I know how. Nedver could be doing with all those registrars they introduced those years back under whatever they as called those new laws. I always were a man for attitude, and you know mine. Ther's the *Apollodorus* to recaulk this winter, and she needs new sails. I said when last I written that I was of a mind, grant Neptune, to be safe home with you for the festival of Cybele. We made our journey with our passengers like what I wrote to you we would, but then I did set off on another one with one of them alone and now he wants me to take him on another one, though he won't say where but the money's good and real. I should know. Near broke a tooth on it. If we go south as I suspects, I'll bring you home a parakeet, and anyhows I'll see you in a while. I hopes the cows are in good milk, and all the kids are well. Your husband, Trimalchio.

From Hanno's memoir

Bostar told me a week later after supper, as he mopped the last of the olive oil from his pewter plate with the heel of the barley loaf Arxes had made and drained his cup of wine. 'We leave tomorrow, Hanno, by first light.'

'Leave? For where?'

I remember how he smiled for the first time since he had come back, even if it was brief and wry. 'We leave, Hanno, for Carthage.'

'Carthage!' I blurted out. 'Why are we going there?'

'Hanno, Hanno, whose son are you? I know your Punic isn't up to it yet, but it's time we got you home.'

'My home is in Capua, with my mother and Labienus and—'

'And? I know. Artixes.'

'Artixes! Why do you mention him? Bostar, what have you got planned?'

'Nothing improper,' he almost smiled. 'On the contrary, I would say.'

He got up from the table and paced back and forth. 'I know, Hanno, how you feel about Capua. But your life was set from the moment your father, with your mother, conceived you there. You are a Barca, of the longest line in Carthage. Now everything your father hoped for is being crushed by Rome.'

'You needn't preach to me, Bostar!' I had, I remember, leapt to my feet and sent the heavy table screeching across the floor. 'I know my birthright. How do you know I haven't also planned?'

He stopped, and began stroking his beard. 'That's fair, that's fair, Hanno. And tell me, what are your plans?'

'To use this.' My arm trembling, from my pocket I held out my father's dagger on my palm. I had slept with it since the day Bostar said it was mine. The tiny scorpion, the Barca signet, inlaid in ivory on its handle, burned in my mind.

'I see. And who will you use this dagger on?'

'On Cato, of course. It's he who has – who did—' I felt the tears come. Suddenly Bostar was beside me, and round my shoulders I felt his arm.

'Hanno, Hanno, you are everything I hoped for, and more. But kill one Cato, and there will be another. Kill him, and there will be more. Believe me. I saw your father. I was at the killing fields of Cannae. I saw what that knowledge did to him. But now the power of Rome has cast off limits. There is no room in her shade. We must—'

'Must what, Bostar?' Suddenly I felt exhausted. Squeezing my shoulder, Bostar turned away.

'Do more. Much more,' Bostar said with what I sensed was some strange pain. 'The ways of peace are harder than those of war. But enough for now,' he went on. 'We have to get up before light, and I have a—' I remember how he seemed to choose his words with especial care – 'a great deal to arrange with Arxes before we go. We'll talk on board the *Apollodorus*. Now, bed for you, young man.'

'Bostar?'

'Yes?'

'Just before I go, two questions.'

He held out his arms. 'Ask anything.'

'One, why does Cato hate the Carthaginians so much? Why did he pursue my father to the end?'

Bostar looked grave. 'That's two questions, and both merit long answers. But not from me, because I don't know. There's a madness that seizes certain men, an anger that will not let them go. Your father had it, but at Cannae I saw it spent. In Cato, I think it will wax more before it wanes. He hated your father; he hated Scipio. Both are dead. To whom will his anger turn? They say he is given to brandishing a fig leaf from Carthage in the Roman Senate these days, and asking if they know that it was picked only three days ago. I—' He broke off. 'Never mind.' He cleared his throat. 'And your second question?'

'Do they have bastards in Carthage?'

This time, Bostar laughed. 'Bastards? Yes, they have bastards in Carthage, Hanno, and in every other place you can think of, with or without a "c". But, Hanno,' he said as he stopped laughing. 'Forget that word, in any language. You are Hannibal's son.'

Letter found among Cato's papers, and preserved in the archives of Rome

My dear son Hanno. I do not know where or how you are, but my love for you is no less strong. Labienus, who is writing this down for me, says that even if he knew he couldn't say. I find my world is ruled again by men. I thought I was free of that. Anyway, there are things I didn't say to you before you went away. When I was pregnant with you, as you know, I was taken away from Labienus' and given the lodging house I still run – and from which Bostar took you with my blessing and my fear. I did not know it then, but my early years with you were my happiest ones. You remember them, and the man I later married, though he died when you were small. Cherish both memories. I thank Juno, and all the darker gods that I have known.

The war with Hannibal went on. I knew who your father was, but like Labienus, like Artixes, I did not say. They were waiting, I think, to see – looking up at Labienus now I see him flinch, but continue to write down what I have to say to you: that is a mark of this man – they were waiting to see who won. I was waiting for you. Men march to war as women menstruate with the moon. Which is more enduring?

Please write to me. I need news of you as plants need light. Here the days are heavy with the tramp, tramp, tramp of soldiers' feet. They have raised two new legions from Capua alone. And now for each lodger I have I must fill in a form, and leave them each week at the prefecture. It is, they say, the 'new order' of Cato. I have never even seen him. It seems a long way to Rome. But, once or twice each week, in the evening, I come here to the house of Labienus. Hulvio the porter is well, by the way. He always asks after you. Anyway, after Labienus, Artixes and I have talked and eaten, I sit and I dream. I must go back home now, and prepare the porridge for tomorrow's breakfast. I have two lodgers tonight. One is a knife sharpener, and the other a peddler of pans. Labienus is leaving tomorrow on a journey. I asked him where, but I see him smile as I say this because he would not tell me. He thinks he will be gone for several weeks. We will miss him, but pray to Mercury that he comes safe home. I love you. May the messenger that brings you this bring me word of you. Your mother, Apurnia.

From Hanno's memoir

We set off into a still and sullen dawn, the air heavy with the threat of storm, the rowers silent so early, surly and taciturn at the lack of wind. Sitting cross-legged in the stern, Bostar and I ate a last loaf of Arxes' bread, some goat's cheese and figs, washed down from a waterskin.

As the big drum beat, we watched the shores of Macedon sink slowly out of sight. Then, as the swell began to rise and I to regret my breakfast, with a grunt Trimalchio heaved himself down beside us. He was a bear of a man, his great, squat head bald and mottled, but for a few wild strands of long and unkempt, straggling hair. His beard reached to his chest, twisted, filthy, oily, and I remember wondering what lived in there. His face was lined and strained from years of sea and salt, but he had kind and twinkling, blue-grey eyes – oh, and I always remember the particularly rank smell of his sweat. It clung to him like a fog. I never saw him wash, or any of his crew. But as Bostar always says, it's the heart that matters. Trimalchio's was true.

'Cabin fine?' he asked us.

'Yes, thank you, Trimalchio,' Bostar replied. 'I've had more experience of it than Hanno here, but it will do us fine.'

'Bit stuffy on a morning like this, though,' Trimalchio continued.

'That's why we came up here,' I said.

'And how are the men this morning, Trimalchio?' Bostar asked, brushing crumbs from his beard.

'Oh, grumbling a bit. It's quite a squeeze down below, you know, what with that extra thirty rowers you had me hire. They're sleeping head to toe, two to a hammock.'

'Sorry? I had you hire? I just asked you to be sure you could out-run any other ship. You said: "Easy, if I can rest my rowers."'

'Outrun other ships, Bostar?' I asked. 'Why should we have to?'

'I'm sorry, Hanno. I should have told you. Trimalchio has confirmed what I was afraid of. The Eastern Fleet has increased its patrols. And we're just not ready to talk to Romans – yet.'

'But you're a Roman, Trimalchio, aren't you?'

He spat on the deck. 'Tuh,' he tutted contemptuously. 'Ligurian, and always will be. Can't be doing with all this Roman nonsense, and the Republic, and forms, and registers. All Rome means to me is armies – why, I lost two brothers, conscripted they were, in the war against that beggar Hannibal.' Bostar squeezed my arm for silence. 'Yes, armies, and taxes, taxes. These poncey Romans even think they can rule the sea! All I ask is the freedom to do what I've always done, like my father before me. Make my living, and mind me own.' Trimalchio belched, and then farted for good measure. 'Anyway, best be on my rounds. We'll be three days to Athens, six if we don't get wind.'

'We won't be stopping, Trimalchio,' Bostar said quietly. 'That's why I had you load the extra stores.'

'So, straight to Carthage, eh?'

'Well, not too straight, Trimalchio, or you might find Crete gets in our way.'

Trimalchio guffawed. 'As you wish, sir. You're the governor, you're the boss. Oh, and as for speed: if things get tight we could always throw' – he gave Bostar a huge wink – 'those heavy chests of yours overboard!' Chuckling to himself, with his customary grunt Trimalchio was up, on his feet and on his way.

Getting up and leaning on the gunnel, I tossed our crusts of bread into the wake. Seagulls swooped immediately, come as sudden sprites, and soared and scrapped and dived. I was silent. So was Bostar. Then I turned, and squinted into the sun.

'What's in those chests, Bostar?'

'Things we'll need.'

I knew – and know – when not to persevere with him. 'Do you really think we could outrun a Roman galley?'

He spread out his hands. 'I don't know. Because we could use fresh rowers, Trimalchio thinks so. And he's paid to get it right.'

'But under sail?' I persisted.

Bostar shrugged. 'Again, I don't know. But we're carrying extra sails as well. A spinnaker, I think Trimalchio called it, and something else as well.'

'The Roman ships are triremes, though, with three banks of oars.'

'Exactly.'

'So they must be faster.'

Bostar chuckled. 'There are many areas in which I feel my ignorance, Hanno. But the respective merits of ships would have to be an outstanding one. Still, let me pass on what Trimalchio told me: triremes are designed largely for their power in ramming. The Romans make war at sea as they do on land: ram the enemy ship, secure yourself to it by dropping the great, hinged *corvus* onto its deck, and then march your men over. Proceed according to standing orders, as on land. So the trireme is not faster than us, no. Heavier, yes, and much stronger; but slow. At least let's hope so. Now, I don't know about you, but I have some papers to look over. I'm going below.'

'Bostar,' I called to his retreating back.

He stopped and turned. 'Yes?'

'About the Roman triremes. Do you think we'll have to put Trimalchio's theory to the test?'

'That, Hanno, is another thing I just don't know.'

For the next few days the only ships we saw were other merchantmen, some heavy in the water and slow, others empty, spry and high and showing a good yard of gleaming viridian weed and glistening indigo barnacle on their sides. I spent hours looking for them to relieve the monotony of the rolling days, and was surprised when, as soon as they saw us, they veered away.

On our fifth day at sea, after the midday meal I was dozing

on deck. Shouts stirred me. I sat up. 'Astern, astern!' I heard the lookout call. I jumped to my feet. Like everyone else, I looked behind us. Despite the swell, I saw it clearly: a *xebec* coming up on us fast, its patched lateen sail full and pregnant in the wind. It was closing on us quickly. 'Rowers, to your benches!' Trimalchio roared down into the hold. 'You, boy! When they're up, you get down below!' he shouted at me, brushing past to take the helm.

'What is it?' I asked him.

'Bloody pirate. Corsican, by the looks of her. Now, do as I told you.' The rowers had scampered past me. Half my body was down the steps to the cabins when, behind me, I saw the *xebec* jibe and turn away. The sailors cheered. I climbed back on deck.

'Why?' I asked a clearly relieved Trimalchio, wiping the sweat from his eyes.

'Why?' he replied, a twinkle in his eye. He slapped me on the back and roared with laughter. 'Look up, laddie, up to the mizzenyards,' he urged.

I squinted into the sun. Ropes, booms, masts, sails, the usual flags. 'I can't see anything special,' I said.

'The red one. See the red flag?'

I looked again. I saw it. 'Yes, but it's just a flag.'

'Just a flag? That means "plague on board", boy, plague. No wonder even pirates skirt us by!'

'But have we got the plague?' I asked incredulously.

'Of course not. But your Bostar wanted us to travel, as they say, incognito. No one close enough, if possible, even to read our name. So this was one of his plans,' he chuckled. 'And by Neptune it works. I'll vow there never was such a man for plans!'

I learned later from a crewman that the number of pirate ships had risen sharply since the end of the last war between Rome and Carthage. 'Bunch of hucksters those Carthaginians,' he told me. 'But at least they kept the seas safe for trade.'

'Don't the Romans?' I asked him.

'The Romans?' He spat a great, green gob into our wake. 'Only around Italy's shores.'

Letter from Cato's papers, preserved in the archives of Rome

To Marcus Porcius Cato, Censor, in Rome; Quintus Vitellius Tancinus, special legate, sends greetings from Amphipolis in Macedonia. If I understood your wishes correctly, I have excellent news. I followed your last instructions, and went to Athens. Trimalchio and his ship *Apollodorus* had indeed docked and provisioned there. I bribed the Greek – well, he was a Scythian, actually, and a fat one, but he said married to a Greek, the sister of one of their interminable demagogues whose name escapes me, which is a pity, since I know you like to know these things. Anyway, I searched for them in and around Thessalonika. Nothing. I tell you all this, by the way, because my expenses will be large but my effort has been considerable and there may be certain things I have, how shall I put it, forgotten . . . So I moved on to this city Amphipolis. A pleasant enough place. The wine is good, for Macedon, and the women even better. Through the friend of an agent's friend, who owns a number of fruit stalls in the market and has his ear very close to the ground, I heard of a certain villa along the coast a few miles north-east of here, secluded, above its own bay. How deep is the anchorage, I asked? I paid over some more gold. Enough for a galley, I was told. And who rents it, I asked? A foreign gentleman, I was told. He paid six months' rent in advance, in one gold bar.

Well, well, I thought. But your excellency will be impatient to learn more. In short, yesterday I went to this villa, or what was left of it. It had burned to the ground only a few days before I got there. I spoke to a certain Arxes, an old fool and the villa's servant. It had been his night off, apparently. He was with his woman in the local village, asleep, when someone first smelled the smoke, woke him up and he ran there. Too late. It was a conflagration. There were no survivors. Of the two inside, he said, the man called Bostar was obsessed with security and used to bar, bolt and double lock all the doors and bar the windows each night himself, in person. He wouldn't let Arxes do it, it seemed. Well, perhaps the smoke got to them first. Maybe they didn't feel a thing. The point is, they're gone. I'm sure. I poked around in the ashes until I found them, or what was left of them that is. Bones mostly. Those of a man, in what Arxes said had been the master bedroom. Those of a teenager in the room next door. That would fit your description of this Hanno. And near the body of your Bostar I found the remains of two strongboxes, both full of gold bars. I am pleased to be able to report that, although a few of them have melted round the edges, most are mint and whole. Strange thing, though. The gold isn't Roman. There is no eagle on the ingots, but an odd looking thing I haven't seen before. It looks to me like a Syrian sword, though I can't be sure.

But the plot thickens further. In one of the boxes, alongside the ingots there are hundreds of silver coins. Now as you know, coinage is something that interests me. You will remember our experiments with Rome's during the war. These silver coins have been minted in the incuse method: the obverse image, a man's profile, whose I do not know, is in relief, and on the reverse the same head has been struck in negative, the two exactly aligned. That is a Greek technique, or I'm a Ligurian. And if I were a gambling man, I would say the head is that of King Philip of Macedon. If I'm right, how did these coins come to be in the late Bostar's care?

Anyway, your excellency, so closes another chapter in the fight against the enemies of Rome. I will rest a few days from my travails and – with the gold of course, and the strange silver which we can resmelt and recast – then I will return to Rome. Whence again I hope to be of some small service to your august self – and, of course, to the Senate and People of Rome.

From Hanno's memoir

There are things I do enjoy about sea voyages, and others I do not: the mass of sweating, bickering, masturbating men; having to relieve yourself in open view over the side; seeing the squawking gulls swoop to scavenge your floating faeces, unless you have ship's belly and instead you stain the sea; the sudden squalls and showers; the stinging salt; the smutty songs; the interminable salted beef and biscuits; the brackish water; the constant creaks and noise; the reeving restlessness of the sea.

But there is an embalming peace that compensates. I was mourning for the father I had never known, eager and yet apprehensive about what was to come; I was missing the known, but excited by the unknown. In these dichotomies, the sea soothed me; the darting dolphins, the reaching rainbows, the eternal that is ocean.

Under a bleached canvas on the upper deck, Bostar chewing on his interminable *bdellium* gum, we made good use of the time. I learned more of Carthage, *Qart Hadasht* in Punic – New Town. Though it is hardly that now, it was to those colonists from Tyre who founded it almost seven hundred years ago. I mean seven hundred by our solar calendar, of course. The subject of chronology—

[Here followed a long, erudite but recondite exposition on the science of time, and a diatribe on the allegedly cumbersome Roman calendar. The latter from deference to my patrons, the former from respect for my readers, I have removed.]

Actually, despite Bostar's disapproval, I preferred – and still do – the less prosaic story of the naming of Carthage from Karkhedon, a prince of Tyre and brother to Elissa. Their father, King Pygmalion, murdered Elissa's husband because he was jealous of him and thought he had designs on the throne. When Elissa then fled in fear of her own life, Karkhedon went with her. Together, for seven years and seven months and seven days they wandered, and Elissa became known as Dido, which means 'fugitive' in Punic.

In Cyprus they saved eighty girls from sacred prostitution in the temple of Venus. Their ship dangerously overcrowded, they sailed on. At last they came to what is now Carthage, but they had little money left. The native Libycians agreed, laughingly, to sell them as much land as an ox-hide would cover. That settled, Dido cut a hide into the finest of strips and so marked out an area of land more than two miles in circumference, with what is now this citadel at its centre. The Libycians were furious, but kept to the bargain. Its bloodline vigorous thanks to the women of Cyprus, the new city of Carthage flourished and grew strong.

But Dido's was a less happy fate. Again, there are several versions of the story. Either you believe it true that when Hiarbas, the Libyic king, wanted to marry her, Dido felt she could not be unfaithful to the memory of her murdered husband. She persuaded Hiarbas to let her build what he thought was an expiatory pyre. She had it lit. She moved towards it, as if in prayer and supplication. Suddenly, before anyone could stop her, she threw herself on.

Or some prefer another account, better known. Aeneas, prince of Troy, was one of few to escape from the sack of that great city by the Greeks under Agamemnon, as Homer's *Iliad* records. With his father Anchises and some companions, he fled the burning city only to be shipwrecked on the coast of our Cap Bon. Fishermen from the village of Kerkouane found them, and asked their queen what should be done. Dido gave the Trojans refuge, safe from the Greeks here in Carthage, behind its already mighty walls. In time, Aeneas declared his love for Dido, and asked her to marry him. After weeks of anguish about her first husband, she agreed.

But Aeneas' word was worthless. Having had his ship repaired secretly, one dawn he sailed away. From this citadel where I write, perhaps from this very room, Dido saw his ship sailing north in the bay, and her heart broke. She ran to the pyre already built to celebrate their nuptials, lit it, climbed to the top and lay down.

Aeneas, of course, went on to found Rome – although the Romans hold to the preposterous claim that their city was actually founded by Romulus and Remus, who had been suckled by a she-wolf, of all things.

[Foundation myths are fascinating. I see no harm in them, and Rome's are better than many: the rape of the Sabine women, King Tarquinius Superbus and all that sort of thing. It gives the Romans the sense of history they need and we Greeks just assume.]

We Carthaginians know better. From Aeneas to Cato, the Romans have been perfidious through long generations. Ask the shades of the Latins, the Etruscans, the Samnites, the Campanians, the Tuscans, the Volscians, the Umbrians, the Messapians, Fretanians, Mamertanians, Sabellians, Lucanians, Apulians, Paelignians, Marrucinians and other peoples, now no more than names, about the worth of the word of Rome. Ask the Corsicans, Sardinians, the Illyrians, the Gauls, the Balearics, even now the Greeks. Ask all the world, bar Carthage. Rome's is a slavery my father fought with his life, and which among the Romans Scipio Africanus, his uncle Aemilianus and others sought to moderate. When will the cycle turn? Even Scipio, the son of Africanus, who besieges us here, has tried to persuade Rome to treat for peace. But he has failed.

From Bostar's journal

[This Bostar is a polymath without parallel in my experience, and he kept this journal through almost all his time in Carthage. But I have extracted only what seems appropriate. The previous thirty pages or so, for example, concern his complex accounting system – which, I confess, I do not yet understand, nor the references to lines of credit held, it seems, right across the Mediterranean. How did he come by these, or finance the great endeavours he set in train?]

We are making good progress. Yesterday evening we saw the coast of Crete to port. Trimalchio is a meticulous navigator, adept of the cross-staff, even though he dismisses the astrolabe as new-fangled gadgetry. Last night, measuring from the pole star to the fore and hind guards of the Little Bear, I used mine to check Trimalchio's computation of our latitude. To his amusement, our assessments agreed.

I have gone over and over my plans. I can find no fault with them. But there are many variables. Still, the die is cast. Now I can only wait to see which way it lands.

Letter preserved in the archives of Rome

To Marcus Antonius Regulus, High Clerk of the Treasury, from Cato the Censor. How dare you question my authority! I am the elected Censor, and what I ask is well within my rights. What is more, my request concerns a matter vital to the welfare of the Republic. I expect you to comply at once. Have the papers sent to my secretary, Speusippus. He will give you a receipt. To reiterate, I want: (1) the will of the late Scipio they called Africanus and (2) all the relevant bankers' accounts. Of course he may have made deposits with bankers further afield. I have begun enquiries among our allies. But let us start with the Italian banks. Because you will have to order these from the various prefectures, you have three weeks; no more. As for the five Roman banks, I expect these in as many days.

From Hanno's memoir

We spent a week rehearsing it all, with Bostar filling in the blanks; how, after the thirteen-year siege and sack of Tyre by Nebuchadrezzar five hundred years ago, Carthage assumed pre-eminence. The colony became the head, and in turn its settlements spread; Gades and Nepheris, Hadrumetum, Amathus, Tripoli and Empuriae are all cities founded in Carthage's name. Passing beyond the Pillars of Herakles, our mariners established trading posts in Senegalia and the country called Quinia, where the women have children in threes; in Madiria and Canaria; and all these posts became towns in time.

Then, as is inevitable, the territorial disputes began. The first were those with the Greeks of Cyrene. But they were resolved and the agreement between the two states was marked by the building of the Altar of Philenae. Both the altar and that agreement still stand. Carthage has always preferred to resolve disputes amicably. We are a people who need peace to trade, not war.

That trade grew in range and extent, bringing us interests in Sicily especially, but all around. Some of the Greek cities objected to our hegemony. We made treaties with them, or made war. We crushed the Phocaeans and the Massaliotes off Corsica; defeated the Sicans, Sicels and Elymians on land. Our trade flourished; our caravans brought goods from the heart of Africa, diamonds, gold, glossopetri and other precious stones, and our mariners explored our continent's coast.

Our black galleys brought tin from the Cassiterides, silver and lead from Spain, nutmeg and spices from the orient and always, always, from our city's rich hinterland and the Cap Bon peninsula we call our garden, we sold grain and the finest silphium, worth many times its weight in gold; from the shellfish fisheries along our coast, we made and sold the dye of purest, murex purple from the Greek word for which, *phoinix*, we take our Punic name.

We lost some battles with the Greek tyrants of certain Sicilian cities, but after these we agreed to respect their independence if they would ours, and leave our trading routes alone. We became a match for the Greeks in power, and rivalled only by the Persians in wealth. Our ships became synonymous with strength and speed, as quick we say as a wing or a thought; and always at the heart of this empire was Carthage, a ship anchored in the earth.

Then we began to encounter Rome. Four hundred years ago we made our first treaty with the Romans. Under it, the Italian coasts were left to the Romans, and the African to us. The question of Sicily, though, was unresolved, and the treaty left the island as a neutral zone. There were Greek cities there, Roman ones and Carthaginian. These in time the Romans sought to make their own. Our Senate protested. They were ignored, and twice the Roman fleet attacked ours. They sent an army to Africa, but were defeated. Then, leading a mercenary army, my father's father, Hamilcar, invaded Sicily. The war dragged on, with victories for both sides, and under the eventual treaty Carthage agreed to exchange its claims in Sicily for freedom to expand in southern Spain. Again, each side was to leave the other's trading routes alone. Carthage also agreed to pay Rome an indemnity. This meant that the mercenaries, by this time back in Carthage, went unpaid. They revolted. My grandfather Hamilcar crushed them in what we know as the 'Truceless War'.

As for Spain and trade, what the Romans promised they did not deliver. Or, if you prefer, my father Hannibal had a hatred for Rome which would not leave him and, by sacking the Spanish city of Saguntum, a Roman ally, he brought about the second war between Carthage and Rome. Of that he wrote, before he died, his own account. I will come to that later – if Scipio is as good as his word. With his army my father did a thing undreamed of. He crossed the Alps in dead of winter and took the Romans by complete surprise. At the Ticinus, then the Trebia, then Trasimenus he routed their armies, and at Cannae he slaughtered Romans as ripe wheat falls before the sickler's skill. There were as many Romans dead, it is said, as there are stars in the sky.

Only by cowardice did Rome survive. They made an octogenarian dictator. He refused to fight, and for sixteen years my father roamed Italy like a wounded boar. He had won the battles, but like King Pyrrhus of Epirus before him, he could not win the war.

Under Scipio, father of the one whose stars have now crossed mine, a Roman army invaded Africa. My father was recalled and, somehow, defeated in battle at a place called Zama, a bowl among grey and arid hills. Truce was concluded, but not by my father. He had gone away to save his country's honour from a treaty that was neither just nor fair. Unresolved, these issues have rankled, and brought us to where we are today. So is this the third war between Carthage and Rome. As long as any of my line lives, there will be more until Rome is weeds and crows.

Letter found among the papers of Labienus

[At first this document puzzled me. The scroll was of the finest vellum, and its wooden staff was inlaid with silver signets of a Gorgon's head. So it had come, clearly, from a rich, important and probably patrician hand. I unrolled it with great interest. It was blank. When I mentioned this to Scipio last night over dinner, he smiled. He had come across this before with secret military despatches. The letter would have been written, he thought, in a mixture of vinegar and milk. He told me to rub the pages with soot. The characters were still very faint, but I have transcribed them as best I can.]

From Rufus Curtius Flaminius, senator, to Titus Licinius Labienus, magistrate in Capua. Of course I will help you in any way I can. I am not only one of the great Scipio Africanus' executors, but he was my very dear friend. I too have heard from Bostar. Now Scipio is dead and Hanno on his way to Carthage, Bostar wishes to take forward his plan. You do not tell me how much information Bostar has given you. Let me tell you what you may or may not know.

Scipio had, although the world does not know this, a son. After the wars against Hannibal, then King Philip of Macedon and finally King Antiochus of Syria, in his retirement Scipio hoped to find and acknowledge the boy. But then as you know his trial intervened.

If he is alive, the son must be around twenty. His mother was a slave, one Hispala. Scipio's father had her sent to Gaul when she became pregnant, but left her well provided for. *[I must not pile Pelion on Ossa, but this truth of two bastard sons, one for Scipio, one for Hannibal, is stranger than any fiction. The etymology alone is of interest. The Romans take their word for bastard,* nothus, *straight from the Greek* νόθος. *One day I will write a history of the lives of distinguished bastards. I could have pairs, one Greek and one Roman. I am sure Scipio would patronise such a project. He, after all, can hardly repudiate bastardy. Although, in his present frame of mind, he might try.]* I can tell you no more than that the agent entrusted with the business meant to take this Hispala to a village north-east of Massilia called Agreti, which was his own home. I confirm Bostar's instructions. You are to go in search of the young man and, if you find him, bring him to my villa in Rome. I will make arrangements in hope. In particular, and although Bostar does not know of my intention, I will now involve Theogenes, once Africanus' art dealer and friend. He is a man, as you may have heard, of many webs. But above all, he is kind.

With this letter comes the pass you ask for. It gives you all the powers of a legate of a senator of Rome. Start by commandeering one of the senatorial galleys in Ostia. Cato will hear of it, but by then you will be on your way. Tell the captain your destination only when you are out at sea. Seek out the banker Josephus by the western gate of Massilia. The password for which he will ask you is 'Zama'. He will tell you, but Gauls prefer silver to gold. Go well. May Mercury, or the Greek Hermes as Africanus preferred to call him, watch over you on your way.

From Hanno's memoir

I have given an historical sketch so that those yet unborn who might read this will understand and know that, before I got to Carthage, I was prepared. The likes of Cato say the Carthaginians are mere traders; hucksters and charlatans, peddling their wares to every corner of the world. That is neither true nor fair.

Carthage is an ancient and venerable city. But the best proof of that is in the constitution which the city bears. When Rome was a simple monarchy, our complex constitution had been working well for hundreds of years. We had and have a Sufet, first minister, elected by our Senate. Election to that body of three hundred is, I accept, the reward of wealth. I see no harm there, for any Carthaginian, however humbly born, is free to better himself and those he loves. If that leads to a seat in the Senate, good and well. Plutocracy need not exclude the poor. On the contrary, it motivates them to work hard and grow rich and pay taxes, the sinews of the state. Our Senate also nominates the Council of Ten from among its number, and this council aids and controls the Sufet, especially in times of war.

But we have other checks and balances: in particular, our Assembly of the people to which all with even a small amount of property belong. This Assembly must ratify, for example, the election of the Sufet. It has many other powers, such as the right of veto over taxation. And in one more respect this is far superior to the plebiscite of Rome. To vote in that, you have to be a citizen and it is no easy matter to become a citizen of Rome. Even to slaves they doled out citizenship during the war against my father, because of course a citizen must serve. That openhandedness is no more. My mother, for example, though a freedwoman and payer of taxes, is not a citizen: her parents were not Romans. But in Carthage we have always welcomed anyone who comes in peace. As soon as they buy property, however little, they can belong.

Nor does the charge that we are vagrant mendicants accord with the many skills Carthage has given the world and honed. Take agriculture, for example. A distinguished Carthaginian, Magon, wrote a treatise of twenty books on the subject two hundred years ago. Even the Greeks acknowledge him as the father of farming. Carthage remains the granary of the Mediterranean, rich as well in vines and olives, flocks, a fertile place of many farms that stretch for hundreds of miles from here, east into Cape Bon, north, south and west inland.

Or consider navigation. Years before the Romans even had barges on the Tiber, my namesake Hanno completed a circum-navigation of Africa. I have his account here. Now the Roman fleet is mighty, certainly, and something to be feared. But which of them admits that they copied their galleys from Carthaginian ones they captured in the harbour of Syracuse during the first war? And it was from Carthaginian and Greek sailors and merchants that the Romans learnt the science of the sea and of the stars. That—

[Lasting for many pages and turning finally to Carthaginian religion, this didacticism continues and tires. Were I a general reader, and not a scholar, I would want Hanno's extraordinary story to move on. I am an historian, but surely a story is either narrative or it is nothing. If the narrative slows, the story dies. Besides, Hanno writes of Carthage's institutions in the present continuous tense, which implies a future. Yet as he did so their very existence was imperilled, and many were no more.

So I now eschew some of the fat on this capon; I omit the panegyric on Carthaginian navigation, seminal though their skill was; I give only a synopsis of Hanno's encomium on Carthaginian religion, and allow myself a rare comment: Hanno praises the constancy of the Carthaginian gods. From his account they seem to me syncretic, largely unchanged from those of the Phoenicians, a people known as long ago as the poet Homer, at the beginning of time. But like peoples, gods must evolve and change – or die. I wonder if we see in this a fatal obduracy, a canker in Carthage's core?]

The Roman pantheon is confusing even to a Roman. They are always adding to it. And when you leave the towns and cities, you find the countryfolk worship darker, older gods as well. Yes, we Carthaginians have our lesser deities, our *alonim* and *baalim* like Melqart, Patechus and Tammuz. But unlike the Romans we have, unchanged and unchanging, the trinity of our great gods: Moloch, known to some as Baal-Ammon, Tanit-pene-Baal and Eschmoun.

Moloch is our male god of the sky, the city and the sun; Tanit, both Moloch's mother and daughter, is our goddess of the earth, fertility and the moon; as god of healing and of dreams, we worship Eschmoun. It is to Moloch, in the form of an old man with ram's horns on his forehead, that in our tophets we sacrifice the weaker of our children; remembering Dido's passing; knowing there will be more. I made libation to Moloch this morning. Yesterday the Romans ransacked his temple on the hill of Byrsa over there. They will find his anger clear.

Letter preserved in the archives of Rome

To Lucius Valerius Flaccus, leader of the Senate, Marcus Porcius Cato, Censor, sends greetings. I have him at last. No more will Titus Flaminius Curtius be able to thwart me and affront the name of Rome. I have just received word from my agents in Neapolis, and this time even the inviolable Curtius has gone too far. You know how the filthy sodomite keeps his Greek boy, the catamite Caroedes, with him at all times. Well, two days ago in his villa outside Neapolis he held a drinking party 'in Caroedes' honour' – can you credit that? All the local dignitaries were there. In his cups on the couch next to Curtius, apparently the little Hebus said, in everyone's hearing: 'Do you know how much I love you, Curtius? Two weeks ago, when we were in Rome, there was a gladiatorial show. But I missed it in order to be with you, even though I have always wanted to see a man killed.'

Curtius replied: 'Have you really?' There and then he yelled orders for a condemned criminal from the gaol in Neapolis to be brought in front of them. When the wretch was dragged trembling before the company, Curtius asked Caroedes if he was sure he wanted to see a man killed. When the boy said he did, Curtius did not hesitate. He had the prisoner beheaded on the spot.

I am having the necessary affidavits sent to you direct. Speusippus will send you the formal indictment tomorrow. I will be dictating it to him tonight. I want Curtius removed from the Senate at once. I trust you, as Father of the House, will allow me to move the motion in person. This time the voices of the so-called 'Scipionic circle' will be stilled. The Republic will have one less enemy; Carthage one less friend.

Letter from Cato's papers, preserved in the archives
of Rome

From Lucius Valerius Flaccus, leader of the Senate, to Marcus Porcius Cato, Censor. I will do as you ask. But it pains me. As soldier and senator, Curtius has given many years of faithful service to Rome. So what if his sexual predilections are not your own? And will you arraign him because of this admittedly distasteful incident, or because he was a friend of Africanus, and a man who argued that we should treat Carthage with a quality, mercy, which you disdain? And by the way, Hebus was Hebe, and a girl. You meant Ganymede, I presume.

From Hanno's memoir

It was the middle of the night. We were all together on the poopdeck, Bostar, Trimalchio, the mate Casso and I, peering forward into the dark and the waves. 'Any minute now, we'll see it,' said Trimalchio.

'No,' replied Casso. 'I still can't smell land. I think we'll be another half watch.'

'And why's that, Casso?' Trimalchio gave back. 'No point going back to your hammock for that long.'

I was still half asleep. 'See it, Trimalchio? See what?'

'The beacon, boy, the beacon on the sacred, doubled-horned mountain they call Jebel-bou-Kournine. Highest point on the whole African coast. Makes Neapolis' Vesuvius look like a pimple.'

'A beacon? They keep it burning all night?' I asked.

'Yes,' Casso answered. 'All night, all day, all year. They say it marks the soul of Carthage and that, if it ever goes out, the city will fall. God knows how they do it. Must use whole forests of wood—'

'Oil, actually,' Trimalchio interrupted. 'They use turpentine and oil.'

'Turpentine?' I asked. 'What's that?'

'The resin, Hanno, of the terebinth tree,' Bostar answered. 'It is almost insoluble in water, is miscible with alcohol and ether, and dissolves phosphorus, resins and—'

'All right, all right,' Trimalchio interrupted, thankfully. 'What do you think this is? A bloody chemistry lesson? Anyway, boy, the only thing you need to know about turpentine is that you take it when you've got the worms.'

'The worms?'

'Don't you know anything,' he laughed. 'The worms. Tape worms. Bit of turpentine and they'll come slithering out like—'

Fortunately, a spurt of wind caught us. The prow dipped, and a breaking wave showered us with spray. As we wiped our faces, Trimalchio said: 'That's enough for me. Casso, I'm going for forty winks. Wake me when we're three leagues from landfall. You, Bostar? You haven't been to your bunk at all.'

'I'm fine,' Bostar said. 'You're not waiting for the beacon, Trimalchio?'

'No. It's a big one, certainly. But when you've seen one, you've seen 'em all.'

It was astonishing when suddenly we saw it, holding half the horizon, the light reaching, running, rippling towards us across the water and the sky. It held us and it bathed us until we sailed through it, and its incandescence lay behind us like the memory of a sweet and soothing dream. I shivered, though the night was warm. That was the first time I was touched by Carthage's greatness. If she showed all the world the way to find her, how great must be those walls?

'Right, I'm off back to the helm. Three degrees to starboard here,' said Casso. 'There'll be lads up on this deck with plumblines shortly, so mind how you go.'

'Plumblines, Bostar?' I said into the darkness.

'Yes, apparently there are shoals.'

'But even Casso knows how to navigate here. Surely they can't just let anyone sail into their harbour, even guiding them in at night?'

'You'll see, Hanno, you'll see. So will I.'

As the night and swelling ship wore on, the carbon black turned to charcoal, the first hints of dawn, with cadmium behind and alizarin too. We stared ahead. Fluorescent jellyfish floated by. Bostar, of course, knew what to look for. Though I felt like teasing him, I remember, I didn't. He was always prepared. Until now?

He pointed Plane Island out to me on the starboard side, lightless but a mass darker than the dark; then, from the waves breaking against it, we saw the sharp point called, he said, Ras-el-Djebel; beyond that the high prow of Cap Bon, a euphemism for mariners, Bostar remarked, if ever there was one; then the promontory of Sidi-bou-Saïd. It was, as Bostar said, like being drawn into a purse net whose edges gradually close.

Two sailors climbed the steps towards us, carrying their lines. 'Best move to stern,' one of them muttered. The deck was full of sleepy men emerging from below, moving slowly to their places on the benches, dipping their hands in chalk before they took the oars, slipping in the darkness; others, like so many monkeys, were hanging from the yards. Trimalchio was up again and at the helm, whistling some ditty to himself. 'Have you there in no time,' he said cheerfully as we passed. 'Oh, Bostar, before too long we'll be needing what I asked for.'

'I'll go below and get it now,' he said. 'Hanno, I'll need your keys.' From the hook on my belt under my cloak, I gave him the bunch he had given me when we left the villa in Macedon. They were for chests under my bunk which, as he had told me, I had never opened. 'Extra security,' he had said, with a wry smile.

'Sails away!' Trimalchio bellowed. The men went scampering up, the sails came tumbling down. Slowly the boat stilled, swaying with the swell back towards the open sea. 'Casso, oars!' Trimalchio ordered, and then came the beat of the drum. The oars bored. The keel bit. The wake sang again.

The first thing I saw of Carthage was the lights – that now shine, most of them, no more. The beacon burned to port, but ahead, first three and four, then many, I saw lights that were, I saw as we came closer, torches burning at regular intervals high up, along what I presumed to be a wall. The sky brightened behind us as we rowed, vermilion dancing on the water. Ahead, the copper cupola of some temple or great public building glowed. Holding the horizon, the mass of a great city showed.

But, leaning right out across our gunnel, I could see no harbour, only a narrow channel, one ship wide, of lustrous light running between two great moles of blackened, darkened stone. Right across the passage, shining with seething weed and verdigris as the dawn grew, ran a row of clanking, heaving chains. Alongside this, by one rope from her prow to a bollard on a mole, oars shipped, the *Apollodorus* moored.

'Who goes there!' came a call in Punic from along the nearest mole. I could see no one.

'The *Apollodorus*, out of Macedonia,' Trimalchio bellowed back in Greek. 'Friend of Carthage, and no foe.'

'We'll see about that,' the voice called back. 'Do you have the harbour dues?'

'Yes,' Trimalchio called back. 'In Athenian gold.'

'Then prepare. We are coming on board.'

I saw him, or rather them, then. Four men, unarmed, in leather cuirasses and caps, which covered their ears, walking along the mole towards our bow. 'They're not carrying any arms, Bostar!' I whispered.

'They don't need to,' he replied. 'Touch a hair of them, and the *Apollodorus* is no more. Look at the catapults up there!' I had wondered what they were, great frames of wood hanging high above us off the wall.

Because of Trimalchio's back, the helm, the mast and rigging, I couldn't see the men jump on board.

'Go forward, Trimalchio, and give them the gold,' Bostar ordered.

'But they'll want to check the hold,' he countered.

'That's fine. But I don't want them to come back here.'

'So what do I tell them is our cargo?'

'Two passengers, civilians, with words only for private ears.'

Trimalchio squared up to Bostar. His voice had lost its banter. 'Look. It's time you told me. Misleading these bailiffs is not a clever thing to do. I've known captains, good ones, crucified for doing so. So, tell me, Bostar of Chalcedon. It's cost you enough. Why are you and Hanno here?' He glanced behind him. 'And you better make it quick.'

'All right, Trimalchio,' Bostar sighed. 'We're hear to see Mastanabal – in private.'

Trimalchio whistled. 'Mastanabal! The Sufet? You're here to see him?'

'You heard me, Trimalchio,' Bostar said with an edge to his voice. 'So what I ask you to tell these gentlemen is true: we have words for private ears.'

'But—'

'Trimalchio!'

'I know, I know. You're the boss. And for what you're paying, I'd tell them you're the Queen of Sheba, for all I care!' Guffawing, he went on his way.

'By the way, what are we paying, Bostar?' I asked.

'A large fortune,' he replied with a smile, 'but a small price.' In those days I didn't question this most Delphic of men.

The bailiffs searched the hold, and departed satisfied, I supposed. A windlass cranked, pulled back the chains. Shadowy figures in the darkness moved on the mole. I thought I saw an arm gesture to come in. Back at the helm, Trimalchio shouted orders. With the starboard oars, we wheeled, and went in.

I remember the sudden silence, the sense of being sure. I entered a long, straight track from which my life has never veered.

Shutting out the brimming light, the wet walls of the black-stoned moles rose sheer above us, halfway up the mainmast. Our drum was still. The men neither sang, nor talked, nor jeered. Then, 'Steer, Casso, you idiot!' Trimalchio screamed back from the bow as our starboard oars scraped and clashed against one side and the walls threw back Trimalchio's voice. To look ahead I leaned out so far that my head almost hit the wall. But at what I saw, I gasped.

In front of us, light lifting off the water, shadows spreading only to disappear, I saw a vast, circular harbour. It seemed enormous, bigger than the whole of Capua. Only a few skiffs and dories, so early, were crossing there. In its middle, I saw coming closer another circle, but this time of land, an island of docks, each the size of our galley, of hewn stone, cavernous, exuding command.

'It is – it is – stupendous,' Bostar muttered beside me, 'A labour of much love – and many lives too, I shouldn't wonder.'

'You didn't know?' I asked, looking back at him. His eyes were bloodshot. He looked tired. He shook his head.

'I had heard of the harbours of Carthage, but—'

'Harbours, you say. Are there more?'

'Yes, one. This is just the commercial harbour. The naval one is even larger, I was told. It's up another guarded channel, with the same arrangement – a docking island – inside.'

'You say "I was told." Who told you?'

'Africanus.'

'He was here?'

'Of course. After the battle of Zama, when your father—'

'I know about Zama, Bostar.'

'Of course. I'm sorry, Hanno.' In a softer voice, he went on. 'Yes, after Zama Africanus inspected the whole city' – he didn't, actually, as I learned much later. There were certain things that even he was not allowed to see – 'as a prelude to discussing the treaty's terms. He told me in great detail about what he saw. It had, he said, a terrible beauty.'

'But this harbour – sorry, harbours. There simply can't be any in the world so, so – secure!'

'I would think you're right. The uninvited just cannot get in, and won't until boats learn to fly.'

'Has anyone ever forced them?'

'Not as far as I know. The only way would be from within the city. Anyway, it's thanks to Africanus that they're still here.'

'How's that?'

'Many Romans, our friend Cato especially, wanted them filled in, destroyed. But Africanus proposed a compromise to the Senate, and won.'

'Which was?'

'That the Carthaginians keep their harbours, but lose their war galleys. Three hundred of them came out the way that we've come in. Out at sea, they were set on fire, and sunk. But what Africanus called this wonder of the world lives on. Anyway, enough for now. Look. We're about to dock.'

Letter preserved in the archives of Rome

To Lucius Valerius Flaccus, leader of the Senate, Marcus Porcius Cato, Censor, sends greetings. Chide me as your conscience commands. Mine is clear. As for mercy, have you forgotten Cannae, and those who fell there? What clemency has ever come from Carthage? Ours is a great endeavour, in which I only seek to serve the Senate and People of Rome.

For that cause, I have more good news. You will remember my expressing to you my interest in Bostar of Chalcedon, for so long secretary – if not more – to Scipio Africanus. When, as my man Tancinus reported to you personally, Bostar unearthed a bastard son of Hannibal, I was even more concerned. Might this boy become, I wondered, a focus for fresh Carthaginian ferment? So when Bostar took this boy Hanno from Capua and his mother, a freed slave called Apurnia, my worry grew.

It took some time to find them. But they will worry Rome no more. They had gone to Macedonia – why, I do not know – where they burned to death in a fire. A domestic accident. I am closing my files. Meanwhile, I am due at the end of this month a report from our agents in Carthage. I will of course inform you if anything seems amiss. I am anxious to learn that the Carthaginians are not building warships, something which, as you know, the treaty after the last war forbids expressly. Though why I call it a treaty, I do not know. With Africanus dead, I can speak freely. I say now and will say again in public that this treaty was the capitulation of cowards like Curtius. I am looking forward to his impeachment. I do not share your sympathy. He is losing only the rank of senator, not his life. He will be freer to pursue his other interests soon. Think of that as a kindness to him.

Finally, I wonder if I might ask of you a small service. The matter is delicate, which is why I am writing this in my own hand. I do not seek the distinctions of the great families of Rome like yours. No Cato can claim to have been there when Horatius held the bridge. My fathers were simple farmers, and I serve Rome humbly, as I can. But now I hold the office of Censor, one of the greatest of the state. Yet I seal my letters in simple wax, for I have no signet to use. I am of a mind to apply to the Pontifex Maximus to matriculate a coat of arms. Nothing hubristic, of course. A plough, perhaps a vine, to remind those Catos yet unborn of whence they came. Would our colleagues in the Senate, do you think, regard this as a matter of good taste, or bad?

Letter found among Cato's papers and preserved in the
archives of Rome

From Lucius Valerius Flaccus, leader of the Senate, to Marcus
Porcius Cato, Censor, greetings. Has it ever occurred to you that,
within reason, we need Carthage? Respect for her – though not,
I accept, fear of her – will maintain our will, our discipline, our
identity as the Republic expands. As for the treaty, I supported
it at the time and still do. I agree, nonetheless, that we should
monitor its terms. But not through spying. With each payment of
the indemnity we imposed, the Carthaginians have to swear that
they are abiding by the treaty. Trust their Sufet, Mastanabal. I do.
He is a shrewd man.

As for Curtius, I will do my duty as father of the house, but no
more. As for the matter of your arms, every aristocratic family,
however old now, was once new. Some of the reverend fathers
will snigger at you, no doubt; others will agree. Which of these
you regard as more important and so what you do is, of course,
entirely up to you.

Note on a wax tablet, preserved in the archives of Rome

Labienus to Curtius. Word spreads as fast among the Gauls as a rumour in Rome's Forum. Five times now have I been presented with Scipio Africanus' 'son'. I was not taken in. What am I looking for? I will know when – and if – I see him. The village of Agreti was destroyed entirely by Hannibal. Those of its people that survived are scattered to the winds. Your pass is no use here. Africanus' money is. I will persevere.

From Hanno's memoir

We were standing in the dock, the *Apollodorus* alongside. Bostar stretched and yawned. My eyes were wide. High above me, in storage bays suspended from the side walls, were oars and masts and prows and planks – enough to make another *Apollodorus* there and then.

'Well, I don't know about you, Hanno, but I'm hungry,' Bostar said. 'Let's go and see if we can find some breakfast, and then somewhere to stay.'

'Even a bath, perhaps, and a change of clothes,' I added. 'Oh, and what about our baggage, Bostar, and all those chests?'

'We'll leave it all on the *Apollodorus* until we know where we're staying.' Then, looking up, Bostar shouted, 'Trimalchio, we'll be back in two hours!'

The shipmaster leaned over the gunnel above us, a biscuit in his mouth, crumbs on his beard. 'So, had enough biscuit, have we?' he teased. 'That's fine by me. We'll stay put, as agreed, until evening. Then, believe you me, by Neptune we'll be getting out of here.'

'You don't feel safe, Trimalchio?' I asked.

'Safe? Son, I'm a sailor. I don't like holes. But I'll keep to our bargain. And, Bostar, as you asked there'll be no shore leave for the men. See you in two hours. And if you're not back?'

'We will be, Trimalchio,' Bostar said. 'We will be. Come on, Hanno.'

'I don't have my money pouch,' I said.

'That's all right,' he replied laughing and tugging his belt, 'I've got mine. Anyway, they won't want your Roman *denarii* here.'

'You're wrong about that,' Trimalchio shouted after us. 'This is Carthage. They'll take anybody's money here.'

I followed Bostar down the dock and round, up some steps to a walkway above. The studs on the soles of our sandals ringing on the flags, we followed the island's curve, the rounded wall that girt the dock until— I stopped, and gasped again. I gasped a good deal that day.

In front of us, a bridge of stone soared in a single arch across the intervening water to a wide gateway. But it was the wall around, above, beyond the gate that took my breath away. It stretched as far as I could see. From the water's edge it rose up to serried battlements in blocks of blackened, calloused, yet dressed rock each far bigger than me. The wall towered. It seemed to be without end. By comparison the walls of Capua, the only ones I knew, were those a child might make of sand, sitting by the sea; or those the tiny pygmy people might build, those who live, as it is said, beyond the heat of the Hesperides.

'Hanno! Hanno!' Looking back from halfway across the bridge, Bostar broke my reverie. 'Come on!'

The gateway was cavernous, its mouth opening as a maw. Its open gates were thicker than a cloak's length, their outside sheeted in shimmering bronze. I thought: 'No guards.' But then: 'They do not need them here.' For ten strides, twelve, fifteen we passed under Carthage's wall, walking on marble flags. When that opened out at last, we paused, eyes straining at the light.

Bordered with houses, three storeys high, some built of a honeyed stone, others painted white, their doors and shutters still mostly closed and irradiating a brilliant, cerulean blue, a wide street ran up an incline before us. Perhaps fifty yards along, I saw a crossroads. Beyond that, more streets, more houses, and the morning's first cart trundling towards us, drawn by an ox with red and yellow braiding on its horns. I sensed the city stirring. I smelt smoke, and heard cows lowing to be milked. 'Bostar?' I asked quietly, awed, 'which way do we go?' He was looking up at something.

'Away from here!' he shouted. 'Quick!'

I looked up too, and as I jumped forwards I saw the face and hairy torso of a man emptying a chamber pot. He uttered some curse at us as the urine and faeces splashed into the gutter near where we had been.

'Well,' Bostar said, smiling. 'That was close. Now, where were we? Which way to go?' He winked at me, and tapped his nose. He sniffed, and sniffed again, and smiled. 'When in doubt,' he said, 'follow your nose.'

That is how we found the market. We followed the smell of baking bread through streets that narrowed into lanes and soon filled with people, pressing on their way. A few looked at us with mild curiosity, nothing more. I remember a young girl, ten or so, who stopped her game of hopscotch to stare. We were then forced to stand beside her as another cart pushed by. She had a fine, hooked nose, large, oval, long-lashed black eyes, a long scar right across her cheek from her left ear to her chin. She had on a simple woollen smock with blue braiding, and wore a necklace of amazonite, blue faience and carnelian. 'Who are you?' she asked. 'I haven't seen you before.'

'We are strangers,' I replied. 'We've just arrived.'

'Oh,' she said, and stared at me, blinking, open-mouthed. 'Come on, Fetopa!' another girl called out. 'It's your turn!' She grimaced at me, two dimples forming in her cheeks, one above the scar, then turned and resumed her game. We walked on – until I saw them.

Coming down the lane towards us, cutting through the crowds, bells ringing, high burdens on their backs, were three great beasts alongside each other, wet-nosed, long-necked, their tongues hanging, their mouths drooling, their eyes already thick with languid flies. They were creatures of a fable, or a dream, and I shrank back, sudden sweat stirring in my groin, against the wall of a house, reaching forward to grab the cloak of Bostar before me. He turned.

'What is it, Hanno?' He saw, perhaps he smelled my fright, and smiled. 'Of course. You haven't seen them before!'

'Them! Them!' I jabbered. 'What'll we do?' Turning, I tugged at him.

He was before me, firm hands on my upper arms. Bostar, my guardian and friend. 'Camels, Hanno! They are animals of Africa, called camels. Camels! Say it! Think of them as horses. You have nothing to fear!' He glanced round. 'Quick! Against the wall – again!'

They passed by, stinking. Pissing as it passed, one of them splashed me on the shins with its urine which plashed off the cobbles, and I can still remember its fetid breath before that. I have never trusted camels since. Massinissa swears by them. Massinissa? I will come to him.

Such was my first impression of Carthage; the familiar, the foreign, the bizarre. The walls, the streets, the houses gave the vessel form; inside it seethed and boiled. The people seemed to come from all the corners of the earth. Large and little, fat and thin, old and young, there were some as black as ebony, as brown as earth; aureate like melons; yellow like corn; as white as alabaster, as sallow as an olive skin. Their hair was of all the colours, some I had not seen before, auburn, red, and blonde. From Capua I was used to togas, tunics and smocks, all in a narrow range of shades of white and brown. As the lane opened out into a huge marketplace, the different colours and styles of clothing defied my senses. I saw a lithe black woman, with naked, small, pert breasts, and golden bracelets on her arms, leading a puma on a leash. There were musicians, jesters, hustlers, traders, men squatting in groups and chewing what I came to know as betel that some call areganut, and others chunam, and all this swelled into one cacophony of sound as people haggled over hessian sacks of nutmeg, raisins, onions, garlic and megarian or thin, tin trays of galbanum, stacte, costum, nard and myrrh.

Each carrying two long, swaying planks of sawn timber across their shoulders, calling out 'Make way!' some porters pushed past us, wearing only linen around their loins, sweat sheening even so early on their chests and arms. In a black, hooded cape of heavy wool *[Here the account breaks off. Having been stained by something, blood, perhaps, or it could be wine, the next four pages are illegible.]*

Letter from Cato's papers, preserved in the archives
of Rome

To Marcus Porcius Cato, Censor, Sempronia sends greetings. We
have your letter of the Kalends of June, saying that once again
affairs of state prevent you from coming home from Rome. That
is a shame. Our son Faustus is thriving, and of course he will be
three soon. You say that you will see more of him when he is
older, and you can teach him history, and Greek, so he can read
the poems of Homer and come to understand a golden age before
degeneracy gripped the Greeks. I think, my husband, that Faustus
needs you now. You could teach him of your love – for him, for
us, for Rome.

But I know better than to remonstrate with you. Your duties
are many, your burden hard. I only want to say that you do not
have to prove yourself to me. Have you forgotten how, in the years
after we married, we lived and worked together for the land; rising
together at dawn and working with the slaves in the fields, eating
what they ate, drinking their sour wine; walking home together in
the evening to wash, and eat again, talk, sleep, make love? For both
of us, I know, those were halcyon years. You were a farmer then.
What, I wonder, are you now?

From Bostar's journal

The waiting is hard enough for me. I do not know how Hanno is taking it. I do not ask. He does not tell. Here in this small house we have rented, two streets south of the temple of Eschmoun, we both work in the mornings – he at his Punic, me at my letters, journal and designs. Two of my teeth are aching. I must find a dentist today. I am sure it is the sweetness of the food here, much of it enriched by the juice of, they say, some cane. I must learn more about it. Meanwhile, we have certainly had time to appreciate and digest many different types of fish. Our cook prepares little else. When I have time, I will compose a piscatology of Carthage. Its waters contain many fish I have not seen before.

Yesterday I went out alone in the morning to find a certain banker and ensure that things are as I hoped. They are. The banker, a Cretan, had kept the acrostic of the password Scipio had given him when he made his deposit all those years ago. I must check the Cretan's calculation of the interest that has accrued. But as a rule, in the afternoons Hanno and I walk together round this great city and explore, ignored. Even on the first day I felt safe enough to let Trimalchio and the *Apollodorus* go, as we had planned. People do as they please here, making money by what means they can. New faces are common in this city made for trade, and no one thinks us strange. But there must be guilds, communities. All will be revealed.

I am most struck by five things about this city, four of substance, one of form. First, the walls. Word of Troy's, Jericho's and Jerusalem's great walls has reached us through the mists of time. In Africanus' copy of the *Ephemerides* of the great Alexander, I have read myself of the walls of Tyre which neither the Assyrians nor even the Babylonians could breach. I have read accounts of the walls and fortifications of Askut, an island fortress in the upper Nile, and descriptions of the defences girding Hattussas, capital of the Hittite kings.

But I have now walked round the circumference of the walls of Carthage and, when the guards have let me, have stood atop her walls. Everything Africanus told me is true. The walls of Carthage are without parallel, stupendous. I make their length to be 21 Roman miles, and their height 90 feet. Every 400 feet or so, wooden towers four storeys high rise above the walls whose breadth seems to average 40 feet, though on the seaward side and where they face the south-western plain, it is more than that. It is in these sections, in garrisons within the walls, that the Carthaginians house their horses and elephants. They could and, I imagine, often have housed soldiers too. How many? When I am better placed, I will enquire. What is beyond doubt is that the city could accommodate a mercenary army in its walls without strain on the rest of the city, while its walls must be as inviolable as man can make.

What we have is a city in the shape of an arrowhead, jutting into the sea which girds it on three sides, the wall rising on those sides straight up from the cliffs. An addition to the city, the harbours where we disembarked jut out into the bay. It is strange, but from high on the walls the harbours look like a clenched fist, pointing at Rome.

To the south-west, at the arrowhead's base, an isthmus perhaps a mile wide connects the city to the mainland. I imagine the isthmus is actually a causeway, because there is a lagoon on either side of it, the domain of cranes and reeds and clumps of stunted tamarisk trees. So they would make an aggressor's approach difficult, if not impossible. As for the causeway, it is protected not by one great wall, but three.

A lower outer wall, with cantilevered battlements, defends a wide moat where, a guard told me, the Carthaginians dump the bodies of their suicides. A special breed of crab sacred to Eschmoun lives in the moat, which even in summer never dries out, and feeds on the suicides' eyes. And do you have many suicides in Carthage, I asked the guard. He did not know. I saw no bodies floating, certainly. Perhaps they weigh them down with stones. Perhaps they have no suicides.

The moat itself is guarded by a higher middle wall, whose catapults and towers could rake the causeway with fire. From there, the ground climbs steeply to the final wall on which I have stood.

From front, side or rear, then, Carthage is impregnable, secure – to escalade or battering, certainly. But assuming a besieger could cross the lagoon or, under protective canopies, get enough men across the causeway, what about mines under the western wall? That depends on the moat. It is wide. But is it deep?

The second thing that strikes me is the city's gridiron layout. It is consistent, even in those parts of the city that are clearly the oldest. But I had thought such plans for cities came with the Greeks, Hippodamos of Miletus in particular, only some two hundred years ago. Perhaps Carthage's founders had a Phoenician model of which we do not know. I will ask, when I can determine who might know. Anyway, this layout would make Carthage easy to defend, and hard to attack – assuming one could ever breach or mine those walls. Fighting would be building by building, street by street. Even if that were successful, the belligerent would face the hurdle of the city's great citadel, whose walls of smooth, dressed stone sparkling with malachite rise up some sheer 50 feet from the Byrsa hill.

Next, the buildings amaze me. Even the simplest ones are made of rubble courses, strengthened by dressed slabs and uprights. I believe the technical term for this type of strengthening stone is the Greek word, *orthostat*. Yet I am sure the technique is an ancient Phoenician one. I wonder what the Carthaginians call it. My Punic vocabulary does not reach that far. I must ask. Anyway, all the buildings here are of stone, not the wood and mud and brick that make up much of Rome. This is a city it would take much to burn.

Fourthly, water. Cisterns and standpipes and fountains abound. Are there wells, springs? If so, where does the water rise? Could this be Carthage's only flaw? I would love to meet the city engineer. But assuming the water lasted, in a siege it would be easy to quench any fires that did break out.

Finally, form. There is a sense of permanence, of confidence about this city that I have not felt elsewhere. It is as if Carthage has always been. This is a city that does not tell its past, but contains it, like the lines of a human hand.

For our possessions, the money and jewels in particular, I am not concerned. The one thing everyone in Carthage must abide by, whatever they do, is the law. The city has many officials they call *mehashebim* who are responsible for the order and upkeep of the streets and squares. There are police on almost every corner, and nightwatchmen patrol. I enjoy half waking to their hourly calls. There is a gallows at the east side of the marketplace. Yesterday we saw a thief hanged there. And naturally, this being Carthage, there was an auction of his clothing afterwards, stripped from him before the cadaver was cold.

I wrote to Mastanabal the night of our arrival, now ten days ago. I have heard nothing. Perhaps, like many great men, he has little ears.

*Letter found among the papers of Titus Licinius
Labienus, magistrate in Capua, and preserved in the
consistory of the Capuan courts*

My dear friend. If this finds you at all, I hope this finds you well.
I write only to inform you of where we are: in Carthage, in the
house of one Malchus, by the temple of Eschmoun. As you see,
I have no need of apocrypha. No one from without can harm us
here. So write to me when and if you can. As for us, what we hope
for has not yet begun. Bostar.

From Hanno's memoir

We had gone to bed. I heard the banging, banging at the door. We had no live-in servant. I got up, pulled on a shift and went downstairs. I unbarred and opened the door, screwing my eyes at the torches' sudden glare. Two men were there, both in matching cuirasses of black leather with gold beading, wearing high collars that covered their necks and strange, peaked hats. Both were tall, but of different build. The one on my left had a long, thin face, a high forehead, a large hooked nose that shadowed half his face in the flickering light, and a lantern jaw. The other man was fleshier, with a round face, afflicted with wens and pink pustules, like a suet pudding encrusted with currants.

'Yes?' I managed.

'We are looking for Bostar of Chalcedon,' the taller of them said. I caught the Punic perfectly, though the accent was still strange.

'He is in bed. It is late—' I faltered.

'It's all right, Hanno,' came Bostar's voice behind me. 'I'm here.' Fully clothed, his sandals on, he moved into the doorway beside me.

'You are Bostar of Chalcedon?' The other man, his voice deeper, asked.

'I am.'

'Then you must come with us.'

'And you are?' Bostar asked mildly.

'We are stewards of the Sufet.'

'Indeed,' Bostar replied lightly. 'I have been waiting for you.

Lead on, gentlemen, lead on.' He gestured into the street, and turned to look at me. 'Hanno, good night again. Go to sleep if you can. But please don't bar the door.' With a gentle touch to my shoulder, he was gone.

Deposition, preserved in the archives of the Senate and People of Rome

Lodged by Marcus Porcius Cato, Censor of Rome, on the day before the Nones of August, in the year ab urbe condita DLXX. Acting under the powers vested in me by custom, statute and decree, I had Marcus Antonius Regulus, High Clerk of the Treasury, send me the will of the late Publius Cornelius Scipio, known as Africanus.

I know it is a serious matter to violate the privacy of a citizen's last testament. I did so because we were denied by Scipio's death the answers to allegations made at his trial. Did he, while supposedly on Rome's service in Spain, appropriate gold and silver that should have been lodged with the *aerarium* in Rome? After defeating Hannibal, did he accept bribes from Carthage in return for favourable terms of peace? After defeating Philip of Macedon, did he accept bribes from Philip for withdrawing the legions of Rome? After defeating Antiochus of Syria, did he accept bribes from Antiochus' ambassadors for withdrawing the legions of Rome?

The official fortune left by Publius Cornelius Scipio was prodigious – more than double our own Treasury's reserves. This, I submit, would be reason enough for us to suspect its origins and confiscate it all. But we have a second reason. To whom did the late senator leave his enormous wealth? Apart from some small bequests of a personal nature, he left it to one Bostar of Chalcedon, not even a citizen, a man whose origins are utterly obscure. How can this be in the interests of Rome? Now this Bostar is dead. No will of his has been lodged. Our laws state that, in the case of the intestacy of a foreigner, we must wait for three years. I move that, in this case, we suspend the law and appropriate now what remains of Bostar's estate.

Finally, it is of course now law that no citizen may hold deposits outwith Italy. So it has been since the black days after Cannae, when Hannibal threatened to destroy everything that we hold dear. According to the will of Publius Cornelius Scipio, he deposited gold with bankers in Rome and Capua, but also in Massilia and Carthagena, Antioch and even in Carthage.

I have carried out enquiries. This Bostar had already made substantial withdrawals before he died. I move we confiscate everything that remains, even those sums outwith Italy if we can. I move we place this money in the hands of the Senate and People of Rome.

Letter from Cato's papers

Lucius Valerius Flaccus to Marcus Porcius Cato, Censor. This morning I read with interest your deposition in the matter of Scipio Africanus. If he held other clandestine bank accounts, why would he declare some? Because, you will suggest no doubt, he hoped to conceal the others. That is conjecture, and our concern is law. Scipio was a general, a senator and a consul, whose genius saved Rome. Yes, he had flaws. Do not you, or I? As for the legatee, as you must know that matters not at all. Remember Quintus Horatius Fabius, who left the whole of his huge fortune to a cow? As for suspending the usual laws on intestacy in this case, I have no objection. What I am concerned about is any slight on the memory of Scipio. *De mortuis nil nisi bonum.* Remember that, Cato. After the debate on Curtius, I and the other reverend fathers will hear you move your motion. Move it well, or not at all.

From Bostar's journal

It was quite a night, and not at all what I had expected. Mastanabal, High Sufet of Carthage and as powerful a man as any in the world, in a nightshirt, with dainty damask slippers on, sitting on a bed in a huge but sparsely furnished room. That is what I found after being escorted for what seemed like many stades. *[Out of interest, I preserve Bostar's Greek here, though I leave him the miles he uses elsewhere. A stade is the distance covered by a single draught of the plough, some 600 Roman feet. The Romans count five feet to a passus or pace, and 1,000 paces make up a Roman mile. It is a system more exact, I confess, than that of the Greeks. The same is true of their respective measures of area. But then the Romans worry about how much land they own; the Greeks about what to do with what little they have.]* We walked and walked through the echoing corridors and lustrous halls where torches sputtered and silent guards presented arms to our profiles as we passed.

What I remember most was the repeated motif of the sign of Tanit – a triangle, with a horizontal line across, and a circle above, its tip. It was painted on walls. I crossed several mosaic floors where, ilmenite on white, it was the theme. I walked past many statues of the goddess, different in size but in form the same. I must look into this. This iconography of Tanit is very ancient. But is the Egyptian *ankh*, the loop-topped cross and symbol of life, not older still?

'So, you are Bostar of Chalcedon,' the Sufet said, gesturing me towards a chair near the foot of the bed. His voice was very high and thin, like a bird's. He had a long neck, like a grebe's, and the huge forehead of his oval, bald and venose face gleamed in the light of the lamps. He had almost no chin, and a small mouth which pouted like a fish. Below that was a very fat body. Where his nightshirt ended, I saw rolls of fat around his ankles. He raised a languid hand.

'An interesting city, Chalcedon. I went there many years ago. Now, wine. Water. Tea, perhaps.' A statement, not a question. 'Yes, tea. Extract of silphium, I think. It thins the blood. Astylax, see to it.'

From the shadows at the head of the bed, from a desk on which I saw a candle and parchment, a much younger man stood up. Dressed in the same uniform as the guards who had escorted me from our house, he was lean and muscular. He moved easily, and nodded a greeting to me as he passed to leave the room. Going by, he gave off the gentlest whiff of bergamot, one of few perfumes of which I am fond. I saw high cheekbones, a strange, flared nose. I could not see his eyes.

'Astylax is my private secretary,' the Sufet explained, moving to sit with his back to the bedhead. 'But his mother was born a Barca, and that makes him a cousin of the late Hannibal. So I thought it would be, shall I say, interesting for him to join us.'

'Lord Sufet, as I stressed in my letter what I have to say is for your ears only—'

'Do not be impertinent, stranger!' the Sufet barked, leaning forward suddenly. 'Next I suppose you will object to these!' He raised an arm. From the room's shadows, four men stepped forwards, in identical uniforms of red. Mastanabal chuckled. 'They, stranger, are deaf and dumb.'

'By nature,' I asked, looking back at him, 'or design?'

'A good question. In Carthage, we exploit both. But you may rest assured that, though Astylax is neither deaf nor dumb, he is both as far as what is said here is concerned. Is that clear?'

'Perfectly clear, Lord Sufet.'

'Good.' He raised an arm again. The men stepped back. The bed creaked. A breeze came through the open window to my left and stirred the lamps. Mastanabal sat back. 'Your Punic is good,' he went on in a more mollifying tone. 'Where did you learn it?'

I was explaining as Astylax returned, carrying a tray. A pungent, fetid smell rose from the pot he bore.

'Good, Astylax, good. And you remembered the honey?' Mastanabal cheeped.

'Of course, my lord.' The voice was deep and pleasant, mellifluous, measured, serene.

'And do you know this plant, silphium?' Looking at me, the Sufet enquired.

'I know of it, yes. I have seen it depicted on the coinage of Cyrenaica.'

'Have you, have you indeed? Yes, its export has made Cyrene rich,' Mastanabal replied. 'It is a strange plant. Did you know that its root tubers have the shape of testicles?' The Sufet tittered. 'Anyway, we are trying to grow it here. We have established farms for it – where, Astylax?'

'Near Hadrumetum, my lord.'

'Yes, yes. Other chamaephytes grow there. I remember, now. That is why we chose the site. I must visit the silphium farms soon, and report to the Council. Make a note, Astylax. Make a note. Meanwhile we rely on imported extract, that costs more than its weight in gold.' Mastanabal seemed to withdraw into himself, to shrink. 'We must find more revenues, more trade,' he muttered, eyes closed.

The lamps spluttered. The Sufet seemed to sleep. I looked across at Astylax. He was looking down. Outside the bedchamber, I heard the muffled coughing of a guard. Suddenly, Mastanabal stirred, rising from his reverie. In a brisker voice, he went on.

'Now then, Bostar of Chalcedon, let me apologise for the lateness of the hour. I sleep little, and by day there is much to be done. You have my attention. You indicated in your letter that you have matters of great moment to raise with me. Whatever they are, I want one thing understood. Rome's spies are everywhere. This meeting did not take place. Is that clear?'

'Perfectly, Lord Sufet.'

Mastanabal nodded vigorously, and his jowls shook. 'Very well then, begin.'

As the hours passed, I grew to like Astylax. His interventions were few, but germane. His knowledge of Rome and her politics was impressive as, at Mastanabal's bidding, I explained why Hanno and I had come.

Astylax had, it seemed, no reason to love Rome. With a Barca as a mother, he had lost much in the appropriations that followed Hannibal's war with Rome. And his father, I learned, had died in the battle of Zama, the last Hannibal had fought, the first he had lost. I sensed that in Astylax I had an ally, and Hanno a friend.

As for Mastanabal, I do not know. He is almost inscrutable. The eyelids close, the smile stays and the thought remains hidden. But in one sense at least I was wrong about him. His ears may be small. But he knows why he has two of them, and only one mouth. Anyway, as I was leaving in the cock-crow and the stealing light, he asked me if there was anything I wanted, anything he could arrange. 'Yes, there is, Sufet,' I answered. 'I wonder if I could meet the city engineer?'

It was for a fleeting moment only, but the arched eyebrows betrayed his surprise. What had he been expecting? Women? Wine? Boys? Chalcedon has a reputation for that. 'The city engineer?' he said, as close to laughing as I had seen him that long night. The smile faded. He stroked his chin and stared at me, hard. 'Who are you, Bostar of Chalcedon, who are you?'

I know a rhetorical question when I hear one. I know the answer. He did not – then. I remember looking at my hands, at my fingernails in particular, and thinking they needed cutting. 'The city engineer,' he continued prosaically. 'Sphylax. My sister's boy. Of course you can. Astylax, arrange it, please.'

His sister's son? Are all these Carthaginians related? If so, this is stronger cement than Rome knows is here.

'Now then, Bostar of Chalcedon,' Mastanabal went on, stifling a yawn. 'You have given me much food for thought. Before you go, are there any other questions you want to ask?'

'As it happens, there is one,' I said, standing up to go.

The Sufet opened his hands in invitation.

'In Rome, in Syracuse, in Chalcedon, in Sinope, in every city I have seen there have been beggars, usually men and women born deformed, or limbless from war. Yet I have seen none here in Carthage. Why is that?'

Mastanabal's eyes narrowed. Tiredness had left him, and he stared at me intently before saying: 'Because, how shall I put it, we encourage the deformed to go elsewhere. You will see no mutants in Carthage.'

'Apart from Halax, my Lord,' Astylax interjected.

'Yes, there is Halax,' Mastanabal replied. 'But he proved himself a very special child.'

The next morning, while Hanno was still sleeping, I called two porters to our house and gave them each two silver pieces. They were amazed. I entrusted them with one of the chests we had brought to Carthage, and told them to take it to the High Sufet's office. They asked if I wanted any message delivered as well. 'No,' I replied. 'Just say that this is from Bostar of Chalcedon, and Hanno Barca. The Sufet will understand.' But there are many shades of understanding. Now I must wait to see which one Mastanabal prefers.

Wax tablet preserved among Cato's papers
[The Latin was diabolical. I have corrected the
grammar. The sense always was clear.]

To Marcus Porcius Cato, Censor of Rome, Astylax of Carthage
writes this. You may trust the man who brings this. He will bring
me your reply. I have news for you of great significance, news that
could change the world. I imagine you would want to hear it. Such
news does not come cheap. So I ask for four times my usual fee, in
gold. Send it by my man.

Letter found among papers in the citadel of Carthage

Cato Censorius to Astylax in Carthage. You people always were greedy. Here is half of what you asked for. I will send the rest if your news is as you claim.

Letter preserved among Cato's papers

Astylax to Cato, greetings. I have what you sent, and know that what I will now tell you merits the balance. I must be brief. There is danger here. A man called Bostar of Chalcedon has come to Carthage. He was first Hannibal's mapmaker, then Scipio Africanus' friend. He asked for, and received eventually, an audience with Mastanabal. I was there. This Bostar has brought a young man called Hanno with him. Hanno is, Bostar claims, Hannibal's bastard son. He can prove that, it seems. Secondly, this Bostar has or has access to enormous sums of money. He sent the Sufet a chest after their meeting. I was not in the chamber when Mastanabal opened it, but I must have gasped at what was there. Anyway, Bostar has made four proposals, which the Sufet is considering. He has put them to the Council as well:

1. *That our Council of Elders recognise this Hanno as Hannibal's heir, and that Hanno assumes all the Barca lands, rights and titles that you Romans expropriated after the last war.*
2. *That Carthage repudiates certain of the terms of the treaty drawn up after the last war: namely it should cease to pay indemnity to Rome; it should build a new war fleet; and it should resume its traditional trade to the west, not just the south.*
3. *That Bostar himself funds the building of 300 new galleys of war.*
4. *That, in return for funding Carthage's entire expenditure for three years, Bostar be made an adjunct of the Council and put in command in time of war.*

The High Sufet pressed Bostar closely on his motives. They seem simple. He wishes the Mediterranean to be shared by two equals. He argues that, unless Carthage regains some of her lost power, Rome will squeeze her, as he put it, 'like a press does olives'. He maintained that Carthage was a great and noble civilisation, and that his interest is in justice; not for himself, but for Hanno and for the memory of the two great men he served. He wants, he told the Sufet, peace. *[So, Bostar's plan unfolds. It is, I have to say, a curious one, at best naïve. What are his motives? Perhaps as they seem to be. But although he has the means to influence Carthage, what of Rome?]*

I know what you want; the plenipotence of Rome. I look forward to that, and to the rewards you have promised me. You will know what to do with my news. In the meantime, send me the balance of what was agreed.

Letter preserved in the archives of Rome

Speusippus, secretary to Cato the Censor, to his loyal wife Silvia in Bruttium. When I wrote last, I said I would be home with you for the festival of the Saturnalia next month. Now I cannot come. Cato has forbidden me expressly. There is much afoot. He has an important motion to move in the Senate tomorrow, and yesterday he was rehearsing his speech. A courier came. Cato read the despatch. He erupted like a summer storm. He threw his desk over, and hurled a chair against the wall. 'Speusippus, Speusippus!' he screamed. I was at my desk in the antechamber, as usual. I entered his room. Red-faced and trembling, 'Get me Tancinus!' he shouted as soon as I came in. 'What, Quintus Vitellius Tancinus?' I replied. 'Yes, you fool!' 'But where is he?' I asked. 'By all the gods, how should I know? Find him. Bring him here! Now!' 'But I—' I saw him reach for an urn. He threw it at me, as I ran from the room.

Well, I found Tancinus, in his cups, in a tavern over by the Flaminia gate. They were cock-fighting in the backyard. He came back to the Curia with me, reluctantly. Still, he walked straight in. I overheard the conversation. Cato was calmer, but his voice had that quiet edge I have grown to fear. 'You are an idiot, Tancinus, an incompetent fool. Bostar and the bastard Hanno are alive, in Carthage. Go there. Kill them. Do not come back unless you succeed.'

So you see, my wife, how it is here. I wish I could leave. But Cato would ensure no one else would ever employ me. Anyway, I am sending money with this letter. I cannot come to Bruttium, so you must come to Rome. Bring with you some of that unguent your mother makes. I have developed some strange lesions on my stomach and chest. I think it is the strain.

Letter preserved in the archives of Rome

Titus Licinius Labienus to Rufus Curtius Flaminius. There can be no doubt. From the nose, the eyes and forehead alone, I know that the young man I have with me is the son of Scipio Africanus. His mother, the slave-girl Hispala, died some years ago of the plague. But her relatives, most of whom speak Latin of a sort, have confirmed the circumstantial evidence. When I see you, I will tell you the whole story. It is a curious one. But for now, I am overjoyed. We have an heir with whom we can restore the name of Scipio and achieve the other things we have discussed for so long. The youngster has been known as Nemon among the Gauls. He has very little Latin, but I am teaching him and he is proving a quick learner. He already answers to the name Scipio. I have told him that in time he will be, like his father, the staff of Rome from which he takes his illustrious name.

For now, I must spend some more days here in Massilia. There are certain payments still to be made, and Africanus' former banker Josephus says he needs more time. I will sail as soon as I can and bring Scipio to your villa in Rome. Meet me there if you can, or send word to me. If you know where Bostar is, tell him this news.

Letter preserved in the archives of Rome

Rufus Curtius Flaminius to Theogenes in Rome. My old friend, I have excellent news. Labienus has found the boy, young man I should say, and within the week will be bringing him to my villa in Rome. Alas, I cannot come. You will know of the action Cato is bringing against me in the Senate. I do not intend to gratify him with my presence. I will trust to the judgement of my peers. Flaccus will see no injustice is done. But I regard the end of my position as a senator to be imminent. So act, and act quickly, in my name. Have my lawyers draw up the necessary papers. As principal executor to Africanus, I want all his former assets transferred from Bostar to Africanus' son. As you know, I have Bostar's prior consent. Have the forms of registration completed for this Scipio to be recorded as of equestrian rank, and one who has joined the *cursus honorum* as of right. Let Publius Cornelius Scipio be, as his father's, his names. Use my name, and the signet I enclose. Preserve the utmost secrecy. Cato will hear of this, for sure, but only in my good time. He will find that the dying scorpion can still sting. Finally, keep watch. Be ready to welcome Labienus and the latest Scipio when they arrive. And be vigilant. Cato's spies are everywhere.

Letter from Cato's papers, preserved in the archives of Rome

To Marcus Porcius Cato, Censor, Sempronia sends greetings. Another moon has waxed and waned, and still you do not come. Faustus is well, despite having trouble with his gums. They bleed, and are inflamed. I am treating them with the juice of ragwort, although it is hard to stop Faustus spitting it out. Otherwise we have a new maid, Julia. She has a good voice, and is teaching Faustus to sing.

I have been much taken up with events in the village. Do you remember that veteran of the war against Hannibal, Rufus? He was a centurion in the viiith legion, and survived not only Trasimenus but Cannae. He came to call on us when he was granted his land here. I am sure you will remember. You discussed with him how he had lost his left arm from the elbow, thanks to a wound he received at Cannae, and whether or not our surgeons are always too quick to amputate. Not long after Cannae, of course, Fabius Cunctator prohibited the amputation of wounded limbs. He ordered our surgeons to put away their trepans, knives and saws. We needed, he argued, every single man that might recover, whole. Most did not, but died of gangrene. Enough, you argued, did survive to justify the dictator's decision. But I am only a woman. I do not understand these things. I think only that a wife, a mother, a sister, a friend would rather have a man they love alive, even without a leg or arm or hand, than not at all.

Anyway, Rufus' grant was of good land, as you know. He has eighteen good olive trees, and the south facing slope grows fine vines and millet. So he makes an easy living, even with one arm. That leaves him time. Apparently the village has been divided about the cost of sinking a new well. Rufus feels the water from the old one is brackish *[I break off this letter here. Amid matters of much moment, the attention of great Cato the Censor is taken up by a well. But I include some of these letters to Cato, or parts of them, because they show that his wife, a kind and good woman, clearly loved him – in spite of himself. So do some see things in us that others do not and we cannot see ourselves. Love, like history, is ineluctable but obscure.]*

Letter preserved in the archives of Rome

Lucius Valerius Flaccus to Rufus Curtius Flaminius at his villa near Neapolis, greetings. Well, old friend, it was an interesting day. I have just returned from a leisurely stint in the baths. I needed it. Now the cook you gave me when you left Rome, Fulvio, is preparing capons from my Sabine farm. I like them as you do, roasted, not broiled. Broiled capon gives me bad dreams.

Like those Cato will be having tonight, I would imagine. You will soon hear the news officially from the Senate's secretariat. But since we have a courier going south post-haste tonight anyway – just some damn tax collection thing – I thought I would let you have the news. As of the Ides of next month, the Nones being inauspicious, you are a senator no more. I do not imagine this news will surprise or depress you. Do you remember how, as we fled together from the killing fields of Cannae, we realised what matters in life, and what does not? I wonder when Cato will learn.

Anyway, he moved his motion of impeachment. He did so well, I admit. His speeches are always honed. And he had done his homework, or at least someone had. His secretary, Speusippus, I would think. Precedents, prerogatives, all that sort of thing. No one else spoke, for you or against. I didn't even ask the house to divide. Your demise as a senator was carried *nemine* – or should I, in the fashion of Ennius say *nullo*? – *contra dicente*.

But Cato didn't stop to smirk. Next we heard his motion on Africanus' will. The debate was long and heated. Fabius in particular was outraged by Cato's getting his hands on Scipio's will. Antonius disagreed, and gave his 'unusual circumstances demand unusual measures' speech. You know the one. Anyway,

I let them have their heads. I rather think I dozed as the debate droned on and the chamber grew hot.

I ordered a brief break for the midday meal. We reconvened. 'So, reverend fathers,' I said, 'we come now to a vote on the Censor's latest motion. Marcus Porcius Cato, the house is yours.'

He stood up in his usual place, three rows from the front. He was sweating heavily. He seemed less assured than he had been in the morning. I know he barely drinks, but I would have sworn he had enjoyed a skin of wine too many the night before. '*Patres et conscripti*,' he began, 'as we have heard, the late Publius Cornelius Scipio that some know' – oh, that familiar jibe, Curtius, you know, drawing out the 'some' – 'as Africanus left his entire fortune to one Bostar of Chalcedon. I set aside the question of how such great sums came to be in Scipio's hands. Our debate on that was inconclusive. I pass it by.' Ever the pragmatist, Curtius, is our Cato. I do not like him, but he is hard not to admire.

Anyway, 'This Bostar,' he went on, raising his voice, 'is now, is now, I can assure the House—' here, Curtius, he stumbled. I thought it very strange. 'This Bostar is now dead. An accident. A fire,' he managed weakly, looking down. But he regained his stride. 'I move we confiscate everything that remains of Scipio's estate, even those sums outwith Italy if we can; I move we place this money in the hands of the Senate and People of Rome.'

'With you as trustee, I presume,' Fabius interjected. There were some sniggers round the chamber. I held up my hand for silence. 'Thank you, Censor. Please resume your seat.' I cleared my throat, adjusted my toga. You know, old friend, how I love the stage. 'Fathers, it should be time to move to a vote. But on this occasion' – I allowed myself a long pause that Thespis himself would have been proud of – 'on this occasion, we will not.' I saw and heard Cato gasp, half rise to his feet. The Senate stirred like a disturbed antheap. Again I motioned for silence, and went on. 'We will not, because I have two documents here' – I pulled them from my sleeve, and held them up – 'which make the Censor's motion redundant.' Well, Curtius, I really am sorry you weren't there. You could have heard the proverbial feather fall.

Eventually, Antonius spoke up. 'And, Father of the house? What are they?'

I stood up. 'Both are properly registered, witnessed and notarised. Both carry the appropriate seals. I will of course lodge them after these proceedings with the consistory, where you may inspect them. One attests the late Scipio's son and new heir—'

'Son, son! He had no son!' Pulcher called out – you can readily imagine the scene. My eyes were on Cato. His mouth hung open. His eyes were wide, and his gaze bovine. His shoulders drooped – and then he buried his face in his hands. How readily, I imagined, would he have forfeited your dismissal in exchange for never hearing those two words, 'Scipio's son'.

By then, everyone bar Cato was on their feet, squabbling, expostulating, waving arms. I sat down. Slowly the storm subsided. I let it die. Seats were resumed. I wondered who would make the next move.

It was Cato. He has courage, that I own. He stood up. He was pale; his cheeks were pinched and drawn. His voice was flat and neutral, restrained and controlled. Again the house fell completely silent, all its eyes on him. 'And the second document, father of the house? The second one?'

There is an atavistic power about Cato. He has Scipio's gift, if in obverse. Do you remember how, from the Senate's steps, we watched the Guard march across the forum to arrest Scipio after his trial? He simply turned and faced them, one man, alone. All around, the merchants' stalls fell silent. Even the beggars were still. It was as if the sun had ceased to turn, and Atlas had put his burden down.

Scipio stared slowly, one by one, at the soldiers. And, one by one, their heads fell. He nodded, held out his arms to them as if in token of his helplessness, and his head sank as well. It seemed an aeon later when, as one man, the soldiers, those élite and hardened veterans, looked up, saluted Scipio in silence, turned, and melted away. Scipio looked up, round, nodded again, turned and walked from the Forum, free, the vessel of his power broken, but still strong.

From Cato's voice and visage I felt, I must admit, a similar command – if, with it, a certain chill.

'The second document, Fathers, passes from Bostar of Chalcedon to Scipio minor all that remains of his late father's estate.'

'But this is impossible!' This time it was Antonius on his feet. 'Only a senator could promulgate such a thing.' He span round, glaring at his peers. 'Which of us has done this?'

Into the shocked, bewildered silence, I answered, old friend. 'Rufus Curtius Flaminius, Fathers. It was done in his name, and with his seal.'

Now Cato's voice rose over the hubbub that ensued. 'Curtius, Curtius! He is a senator of Rome no more!'

I closed my eyes and stroked my beard. Did you know I have grown it again? When my colleagues were quiet, I went on. 'That is correct, Censor. "Is". But Curtius was, until this morning. And this deed was executed two days ago. Scipio's son, reverend Fathers, is alive, and will soon be here.'

[There follow several pages of self-congratulation, and reminis-cences about campaigns this Lucius Valerius Flaccus fought with Rufus Curtius Flaminius in Bithynia and Macedonia and Spain and other places that now belong to Rome. Then there are patrician japes about Cato's petition to matriculate arms, and so on. Though an historian, I have preferred to break off this narrative at a point which, it seems to me, a dramatist might have enjoyed.]

From Hanno's memoir

I remember when I met him as though it were yesterday. It was an autumn morning, the wind from the north, cirrus clouds scudding across the sky. Bostar was working. I had done my day's Punic, started out for a walk, returned for a cloak against the chill, and gone out again. As I entered the potters' quarter, not for the first time on my walks I stopped to watch a particular woman at work; both because she was a woman, and I still found that strange because in Capua only men could ply such a trade, and because she was making a huge, deep-bellied pot, larger than any I had seen before. Potting fascinates me. I had become a useful amateur, before this war. In Punic we call a potter *yotser*. The word means 'the one who gives shape to the unshaped'. The Latin word *figulus* is much more mundane. We are all unshaped before the gods' great wheel. Of me, see what they have made.

As I, squatting, watched the woman work, her wheel spin, her hands form this thing of beauty from mute clay as the kiln behind her smoked, sputtered and flared, my eye was caught by movement under a blanket to the woman's right. A face appeared, like a weasel's, the features sharp and pointed. It was a human face, a young man's, yet one that looked old beyond its years. At first, I couldn't understand. The body was on all fours, and yet the blanket over it was humped, like a laden mule. 'Mother, may I go and see them now?' the figure said.

'Yes,' the woman replied, suddenly looking up at me with kind and lustrous, dark brown eyes. 'You can, Halax. But be back for the midday meal. And take this one with you – if he wants to go. Do you want to go with my son Halax and see elephants?' she asked me, her wheel slowing, her hands still on the clay. 'I have seen you before.'

'I— I—. Elephants? Yes, I suppose so.'

'Then follow me,' Halax said. I looked up at him. Standing up, I looked down. He was half my height, his head a shock of curly, ginger hair. He had enormous, red, swollen and ballooning ears whose lobes hung almost level with his chin. But my eyes were drawn, despite myself, to the lump that was his back. I forced my eyes away from that. My eyes met his, green ones flecked with grey, squinting into the sun. They bored into me. 'My mother says,' the words flew out of him like the songs of birds in the morning, 'that it is rude to stare.'

Letter preserved in the archives of Rome

Speusippus, secretary to Cato the Censor, to Marcus Antonius Regulus, chief clerk of the aerarium. My master is unwell. He is in bed, suffering from one of his blinding headaches. Even the buzzing of flies gives him pain. So he will not attend your audit today. I went in to ask him whether he would want you to proceed without him, but he waved me away, and groaned, so I do not know. What I think likely is that he will chastise you whether you proceed without him, or whether you do not. I leave the choice to you.

From Bostar's journal

At least they came by day this time, the stewards of the Sufet. And they were different men. Perhaps stewards were allowed time off – something Mastanabal did not seem to grant himself. It was almost a month after my nocturnal meeting. 'The High Sufet Mastanabal bids you join him the day after tomorrow for a boar hunt,' one of the stewards intoned, rather than said. 'And the boy Hanno is to accompany you.'

'Boy?' I replied. 'He's hardly that. He—'

'The boy Hanno is to accompany you.'

'All right. But a boar hunt?'

'A boar hunt. A litter will call for you both just after first light.'

'A litter? We can walk. I've never—'

'A litter will call for you just after first light.' In unison, this pair of martinets bowed their heads at me, turned and retraced their measured way.

Letter found among Cato's papers, and preserved in the archives of Rome

My dear mother. It has been nine months now since we left, and still I have not heard from you. Please write to me, and tell me you are well. How is the boarding house? I hope the taxes are not too high. I could send you some money. At least I could ask Bostar to. He has much of it, in chests in our house. Write to me, soon. If you have difficulty with the characters, I am sure Labienus or Artixes will help you write down what you feel. Please tell Labienus that I am thinking of him, and Artixes too. I wonder how you all are.

Bostar and I are in Carthage. Bostar says we are safe. You can send a letter to me here, at the house we have rented. Tell the courier you use that it stands second last on the left before the potters' quarter, near the temple of Eschmoun. *[Here there are marks from a different hand in the margin, and these last words are underlined. I can only assume, since I found this letter in Cato's papers, that it never reached the widow Apurnia, and that these marks are Cato's, or one of his men's. So much love in life gets lost, or does not reach its end.]* We have a servant who cooks and cleans. Bostar works mostly, and says he is waiting for a message. About what, he will not say. I do know that he went to see someone they call the Sufet. He is a kind of king. But you know how Bostar always has plans.

The weather is much like it was in Capua. The language, Punic, is strange, but I have learned a great deal. I was lonely here at first, but now I have a friend. His name is Halax. He is a hunchback. He took me to see extraordinary creatures they call elephants. They are huge, ten times bigger *[four, I would say.]* than the biggest horse, and live in stables within the city walls – which gives you some idea of how big the walls are. *[This hyperbole as to the elephant's size is, I suppose, inevitable in one as young and impressionable as Hanno was then. But he was referring, of course, to the African elephant, not the Indian. The former differs from its cousin in being bigger, having larger and triangular ears, a concave back and a more segmented trunk. Readers who wish to learn more of this great mammal should refer to Aristotle's seminal work, De Partibus Animalium.]* Some of the elephants have tusks, and they all have long trunks with lips at the end of them and very large ears. They drop steaming turds bigger than my head. I was scared, but Halax talked to these elephants. He said they are gentle, and just as intelligent as men. I asked him how you could tell them apart. He said: 'Look at their ears. They are as different as human faces.' I peered up, and began to see what he meant. As I did so, I am sure that one of them, a huge cow called Ruba with a broken tusk, winked at me, raised her trunk and smiled. I stroked her belly. The skin was as thick as a leather cuirass.

The Carthaginians use these elephants to carry great burdens around the city: stones for building, merchants' wares. Halax says they are much used in forestry, dragging whole trees out by the roots in the forests south of here and then carrying as many as three trees down to the nearest road. He says my father had elephants with him when he invaded Italy. Is that true? How could they have survived the Alps, the cold and the snow? I must ask Bostar. He will know. Write to me, please. Your loving son, Hanno.

From Bostar's journal

Mastanabal has proved as good as his word. I have now met Sphylax, a scholar and a fastidious young man for whom engineering is not just a science, but an art. He works from offices in the Council's building, in the shadow of the citadel. He was reserved at first, but soon warmed when he saw that my interest was genuine. I was wrong about the walls. More accurately, I was ignorant. Sphylax has promised to take me on a tour of them tomorrow, to show me what he explained. It is all, apparently, in the joints. How do you join hewn stones to make them impervious to battering rams, even ship-borne ones like Alexander used against the walls of Tyre?

Sphylax's father, it transpired, was responsible for supervising the rebuilding and strengthening of most of Carthage's seaward walls while Hannibal's war dragged on. I learned that the huge cost of this, and the higher taxes that resulted, added to the case of the so-called 'Peace Party' – those in Carthage who thought that Hannibal should be recalled and peace made with Rome. So it is even smaller wonder that Hannibal never had the men or munitions from Carthage for which, so often, he called. So do I put flesh on the bones of great matters in which I was involved.

Anyway, Sphylax's father used as his model the work of Dionysius of Syracuse, and his great wall at Epipolae that no one has ever broken down. Here I was on firm ground, for I have often seen this wall, when I was a merchant's clerk, many years and lives ago. Sphylax's enthusiasm, though, was that of a master, and mine merely that of an acolyte of the trade. Dionysius' engineers – their names, sadly, are lost to us – designed a casemate wall with, if my Punic served me well enough, what Sphylax called an innovative 'chain masonry' technique: every 10 to 20 feet, rectangular stones alternated as headers and stretchers. The headers reached through the fill to the opposite facing wall, connecting the two walls and making them, Sphylax insisted, 'as strong as natural rock'. Carthage's walls are made in the same way. I hope we never have to find out whether Sphylax's confidence in their strength is right or wrong.

He turned next to defensive arms, catapults and onagers and the bows known as gastraphetes in Greek – 'belly bows'. But here I had to confess my ignorance. Sphylax was disappointed, but promised to instruct me in this arcane art.

I changed the subject to another vital one – water. Carthage had, I learned, no crucial sources or springs a besieger might foul, not even the most vulnerable of supplies, an aqueduct. Instead, she relied on great underground cisterns, filled by the winter's rains. How big, I asked? He laughed. 'This city would have water,' he said, 'even if it didn't rain for the next ten years.'

Measuring supply is easy. But demand? That would rise or fall, depending on fires or deaths. Still, I took Sphylax to mean that the city's water was secure. I brought up the question of grain stores. An assistant interrupted us. Before he could answer me, Sphylax was called away. The question of filling Carthage's bellies will have to wait for another day.

Marcus Porcius Cato, Censor, to Spurius Lingustus. Your colleague Quintus Vitellius Tancinus is unavailable. Come to my offices. Draw as much money from Speusippus as you need. Hire four men, no more. Watch every boat that lands at Ostia – especially those from Massilia. One will have a young man on board, now known as Publius Cornelius Scipio, although he may not yet use that name. He is Africanus' bastard son. He should be accompanied by a minor Capuan magistrate, one Titus Licinius Labienus.

I want to know as soon as they are here. I want to know where they stay. The villa of Rufus Curtius Flaminius, until lately a senator, would not surprise me. You will know it well. I hope the porter is still in our pay. If not, see to it.

So, find this Scipio. Watch him, every minute of the night and day. I want a report, written or spoken, at dawn and dusk each day.

Letter preserved among Cato's papers

Furius Bibaculus to Marcus Porcius Cato, Censor, greetings. I have yours of yesterday. You refuse to allow me to buy more slaves for this project, saying I must work the ones I have even harder. Very well. But do not be surprised if many die. I am already working them 18 hours a day, as you ordered, digging by torchlight when the sun sets. The tanks will be ready by next week. The dressed stones are here to have them lined. Then we should fill the tanks with water the week after, and bring in the fish. If they breed as fast as we believe they will, the carp from Rome's first fish farm should be ready for market with the first winter rains – just as the natural supply begins to fail.

So, if the slaves' strength is sufficient, our project will be complete on time. Our neighbour here, Quintus Valerius Gracchus, continues to complain. You know he built a summer house at the foot of his garden, overlooking our ground. He says the noise of construction disturbs him, as does the slaves' smell if the wind is from the north. He says we should not have been allowed to build a farm for fish so close to Rome. But as you know, for reasons of transport that proximity is critical to our plans. So please seek to mollify Gracchus. You will know the best means for the man.

From Bostar's journal

I must admit to a certain satisfaction. I received a letter from Labienus this afternoon. He has found Scipio's son, and the two of them are in Rome. My plan is unfolding. *[This naïvety again: there is the fable of the shepherd who found what he took to be an abandoned puppy. He trained it, and it tended his sheep until, one day, it killed them all. The puppy was not a dog, but a wolf. How can Bostar know that Scipio will be accepted? If he is, will nurture be greater than nature? The latter might prefer not peace, but war.]* I will write to Theogenes, and reply to Labienus, now. My sense of well-being grows. Only this morning, as I was walking back from the barber's in the market, I witnessed a crime. A well-dressed merchant, his retainers about him as restless remoras attend a shark, was walking in front of me. He paused and turned to talk to someone he knew, and some ruffian in a patched green cloak brushed against him. 'My purse, my purse!' the merchant bellowed as the other darted down the lane to our left. Well, within seconds, *mehashebim* and police were on the spot. By the time a crowd had gathered, the culprit had been led before the merchant, and the latter's purse returned. The criminal, I understand, will lose his right hand. That is the punishment. *[It will have been the left hand, actually, for a first offence. I have the Penal Code of Carthage here, rescued from the citadel, and I have read it with some interest – and disdain.]* This incident confirms my feeling that we are safe here. I am sure that I can execute my plans.

From the journals of the Senate and People of Rome

Let it be known that from this day, a.d. xii Kalendas Mart. a.u.c. dlxxi, for distinguished service to the state and having undertaken the lustrations required by law, Quintus Valerius Gracchus is elevated to the equestrian order, with all the rights and responsibilities this commands, and is as of this day so recorded in the census of Rome. Executed under the seal and authority of Marcus Porcius Cato, Censor.

Letter preserved in the archives of Rome

My dear Curtius. They have arrived safely, and the young Scipio graces your villa here in Rome. I must thank you for getting me involved. He is his father's son, no doubt. There is much of Africanus in his mien. There is a great deal he needs to learn – his table manners, for example, are atrocious – but we will teach him in time. He is tall, and lithe, and well proportioned, though I would say his arms are a little too long. His forehead, eyes, high cheekbones and nose are his father's. His full mouth and sandy hair are, I must suppose, from his mother – but I will pass quickly on. He looks strong and healthy. Even his teeth seem fine. I will take him to the baths with me tomorrow and then we shall see more. His Latin is rudimentary, and of course he has no Greek at all. He and Labienus converse in a Gaulish–Latin pidgin, which makes a disagreeable sound. But underlying that, he has a voice like a lyre and a laugh that sings. Indeed, were he not who he is and these times not as they are, I should be very tempted to claim this Ganymede for my own. What, I wonder, are we to do with him? Or do you want me to take him under my wing, show him some art and dally the days away? Theogenes awaits your instructions, as he always enjoyed those of Africanus, extol that numinous name.

Letter preserved in the archives of Rome

Curtius to Theogenes. I am writing this myself, by return courier. He is neither colt nor *kouros*, by all the gods. Get him a tutor, for a start. Try that man Ennius. He lives on the Aventine somewhere. He's a Messapian, but they say he's good. And he's a client of Cato's, so at least there's irony here. I want Scipio's Latin perfect within three months. In fact, get him several tutors. Ennius for language, another for background and manners, a third for arms. Can your charge use a sword? Does he know a *pilum* from a postern? I assume that he can ride. Gauls learn to do so before they can walk, and I presume that is how he was reared. But check. Do not, I repeat, do not take him with you to the baths. Have the slaves wash and strigil him at home. Make sure he stays within the grounds of the villa until I say otherwise. I may no longer be a senator, but I believe that I still have friends. There is much to be done. Send Labienus to me here near Neapolis. Tell him to use the horses of one Demodocus. He will find his livery by the Fulvian Gate.

From Hanno's memoir

It all happened so quickly. Bostar and I had gone down into the
market that afternoon. Bostar's teeth were hurting, and had been
for some time. We were looking for a dentist, and kept being sent
down narrower and narrower lanes as we sought the premises of
a Scythian called Monodos – not, I admit, the most auspicious
name. I look across this crowded room now, as smoke from the
burning city wisps across us all and stings my aching eyes. I see
Bostar, bent over a small writing table in the corner and, in spite
of myself, I smile. For love, for laughter past, for loss. I both mourn
and celebrate what has been, and all that might yet be.

Bostar was in front of me. The lane was narrow, and houses
towered above us on both sides. From the shopfronts, traders
besought and begged us to sample their wares, to buy their ostrich
feathers, paraetonium, tree moss, thyon wood, cumin, pulses,
murex, truffles as, all around, the smoke of charcoal filled the
air. 'Come on, Hanno!' Bostar shouted cheerfully, looking round.
'Look. This Monodos must have his surgery just down there!'

Two hundred yards ahead, I saw, the booths stopped and the
lane was still, its houses broken by alleyways and hydrants. I
quickened my pace, slowed to sample the smell of a bay of
apricots, stepped out again and was almost upon Bostar – when
he was gone.

I ran forwards quickly, puzzled. I was too old for children's
games. To my right, down a dark vennel, I saw two shapes,
struggling. One I knew was Bostar by his ochre cloak. The
other? I saw the gleam of steel, a knife in the other shape's
right hand as Bostar wrestled to break free from the left forearm
across his throat. If it is a madness, it is a divine one, and I

praise Tanit-pene-Baal. I fumbled for it, found my father's dagger, launched myself at both of the bodies and, as we all fell, thrust it thudding home. My arm reaching round him, I lay on Bostar's front, and he on top of another whose throes convulsed him. My face fell on that man's. I smelt his fetid breath, felt his stubbled chin and I saw the flecks of blood blowing in bubbles round his lips and I remember thinking, as the sweat coursed from me, they were very beautiful until I realised that, as his resisting eased, I had killed a man.

I do not know how long we lay there. My fingers loosened on the dagger's grip. I pulled it out. The man exhaled and groaned and I reached the dagger up again to plunge, to plunge—

Bostar stopped my fatal arm. Awkwardly he rolled over, off the man, still holding my arm and I sat up, panting. 'It's all right, Hanno,' Bostar said, raising himself on an elbow. I felt the stickiness on my right hand, and I held it up to the light. Excrement, human faeces. We had been lying in an open sewer, and I looked at my hand and laughed, laughed, laughed – until Bostar shook me, and I was still. I stared at him.

'Is he, is he dead?' I managed.

'Either dead, or nearly,' I think Bostar replied, struggling to his feet. 'We must call the *mehashebim*, quickly. Get up Hanno.' I did, feeling faint and cold and beginning to tremble. I looked down. There was no movement from the man.

'Do you recognise him?' I asked.

'No,' Bostar replied dryly, 'but I barely have his acquaintance. Hanno?'

'Yes?'

He looked at me, eye to eye, and said, simply, 'Thank you.' He shook himself.

'Now, give me that,' he said, pointing at the dagger. I handed him the blade that had been my father's. He held it up before him. 'So,' he said, 'do greater designs unfold than we can guess at. I brought this dagger for you as a keepsake. Now it has saved my life.' Then he muttered something in a language I did not know, briskly wiped the dagger in a fold of his cloak, spat on it, wiped it again and gave it back to me. 'Put that away, Hanno. Now, come on. The *mehashebim*.'

They were not hard to find. We led them to the vennel. Their whistles sang. The police arrived. We told them what had happened. The body was carried away. We were escorted back to our house, the guards at first pushing through the curious crowd that had gathered and, seeing no more excitement and this being Carthage, soon melted away.

'Court house, second watch tomorrow morning. House arrest until then,' one of the policemen ordered as Bostar opened our door. Bostar turned. 'For an enquiry?'

'Yes, preliminary hearing, anyway. Now, get in. You two,' he said, gesturing at two of the junior guards, 'stay here. No one out, no one in.' Then, turning to us, 'Right, inside,' he said, utterly matter of fact, almost bored, his voice mellifluous and mild. Despite the deep pock marks he had a kindly face, this *echataz*, a rank like the Roman tribune, I suppose.

Turning as I followed Bostar, I caught the man's eye. 'The man?' I asked him.

'Who?'

'The man. The man I— is he dead?'

'You'll find out in the morning. Now, close the door.'

From Cato's papers

Marcus Antonius Regulus, High Clerk of the Treasury, to Marcus Porcius Cato the Censor. As you know, I have had fresh probate served in the matter of the will of the late Publius Cornelius Scipio, known as Africanus. He now has a son and heir, and all Africanus' assets pass from Bostar of Chalcedon to Publius Cornelius Scipio, Africanus minor. I am seeing these matters settled, as is only just and fair.

But as it happens, two things have since come to light of which I think you should be aware. Only yesterday did I receive a reply from one of our Roman banks to my request for information. That of the bank of Figulus in Padua is astonishing. The late Africanus had 200,000 gold staters lodged there. The amount of itself is remarkable. No Roman can ever have possessed so great a sum before. What is more, though, the staters are Syrian. They bear the head of king Antiochus himself. So perhaps the rumours of how our invasion of Syria ended are true, and Africanus was bribed to end the war. But if this is so, there is nothing you can do. I need not tell the Censor of our statutes of limitation. Nor need I express my indignation at what seems to have been the perfidy of a great Roman. I had always assumed your animosity towards Africanus to have been born of spite if not indeed, if you will forgive me, jealousy. It appears that I was wrong.

The second matter is even graver. I collated Africanus' will and other papers personally. I wanted the new affidavits lodged with them. In the process, I came across a document I had not opened before. You will remember, Censor, the sudden spate of child prostitution that disgraced our great city some nine years ago? At first it was Spanish boys and girls; then Syrian; then Greek. I remember your many speeches on this canker at Rome's core. All our ports were watched, our borders, each of Rome's gates, but still the children came. You thought Rufus Curtius Flaminius was involved. You tried to have the art dealer Theogenes arrested as the originator of this evil trade, but never could find hard evidence. I have it now. Africanus was the presiding force. I have, in his own hand, a ledger: children bought abroad for pennies or trinkets, then sold for golden *denarii* in Rome.

So now we know, in part at least, how Africanus equipped at his own expense the Roman army that invaded Africa and defeated Hannibal. *[It is fitting, I suppose: through child prostitution Rome was saved, and here is matter worthy of my countryman Diogenes.]*

From Hanno's memoir

We did find out, of course. The justice of Carthage is swift and sure. I remember asking Bostar nervously, as we walked into the huge echoing hall of the court the next morning, if he had ever been in a court before.

'Yes,' he replied. 'I was present at the trial of the brothers Scipio in Rome.'

'Of course. But were you ever on trial in person?'

He smiled. 'Yes, I was once. In your home city.'

'In Capua?' I blurted out. *[I have already expressed my admir-ation for this Bostar's mind. But perhaps one has to extend that to his eclectic and interesting life. Apart from this journal of his time in Carthage, which of course I am excerpting, I wonder if he kept a record of his life before he went there? Might he have written, for example, of his time with the great enigma Scipio Africanus, saviour of Rome despite himself it seems? I will widen my enquiries.]*

'Silence in court!' bellowed a bailiff. We had come before the bar.

What I remember is majesty, awe. Something greater than us, than people yet unborn, law. The judge sat high above us on a huge cathedra of gopha wood inlaid with precious stones, spinel, the eighteen colours of topaz, beryl, tourmaline and star sapphire. Under his tall, triangular hat of light purple bearing the sign of Tanit in gold, I could not see the judge's face. But his beard reached to his chest. His robes were deep murex purple, and four clerks sat below him, their tunics of brightest woad, their parchment and pens ready.

Between us and the bar was a table, topped with white marble.

On it was the first water-clock or *clepsydra* I had seen, its keeper sitting by its side. Its calibration was matched carefully, Bostar had told me, with that of the city's twelve *clepsydras* in the temple of Eschmoun. The time the bowl takes to sink we know in Carthage as one *paya*, and day and night we divide into 30 *paya* each. Any case – I knew because Bostar had told me – which lasted more than three *paya* was adjourned, and adjudicators appointed to each side to determine the facts of the case and present them to the judge.

The room was vast, its roof one great arch, and through its cupola the light streamed. The dust mites soared. Law. An abstraction? No. A natural, atavistic verity. Our word *lagu* means 'what lies fixed, or even'. The law gives form to that. *[This is puerile. Yes, there are laws which draw their force from nature. Incest, for example, is rightly prohibited in every society of which I know. But most laws are of course legal. The Romans, for example, drown in their interminable property laws, while the Spartans' laws cannot be called laws at all. Does the* helot *in Sparta give his or her consent to be a slave? Is a law which is not in the interests of the whole community truly a law? In any case, the concept of natural law cannot elude the question of whether moral propositions like 'right' and 'wrong' can be known as true. Law is no more than a product of human reasoning. So, like its makers, it can only be understood within four sets of order: natural, logical, moral and cultural.*

I have studied the Carthaginian legal codes, as I have said. The admirable interspersions of the Sufet Hararabi are proof to the rule. Barbarous and simple, these codes' field of reference is only the first of this four. So I pass by Hanno's encomium on them. Is it perhaps in their failings that lay more seeds of Carthage's fall? To know a people, study their laws.]

'Keeper, start the clock. Prosecutor, begin,' intoned the judge, almost uninterested.

To our left, a tall man in a blue shift rose from his seat, and cleared his throat.

'A simple case, your honour. Attempted murder. A Roman

citizen, one Quintus Vitellius Tancinus, came to Carthage to murder the two before you: Bostar of Chalcedon, and Hanno of Capua.' Hanno of where, I wondered? Hanno, son of Hannibal, Hanno Barca. But Bostar had told me to say nothing unless asked specifically.

'And this Tancinus?' the judge enquired.

'Wounded by Hanno in defence of Bostar, sir, but alive.'

Beside me, Bostar exhaled deeply. I felt – what did I feel, those many years ago? I had not meant to kill him, just to save Bostar. The judge went on. 'Can he come before the court?'

'He can, your honour,' the prosecutor replied. 'Bailiffs, bring him in.'

Both Bostar and I turned to watch a stretcher being carried into the court. On it lay a man, covered by a blanket, black-haired, sallow skinned, with narrow eyes crowned by bushy eyebrows. Beads of sweat glistened on his forehead, and on the stubble of his chin. His breathing was laboured as he lay, stertorous and rasping.

'Put him down, bailiffs,' the judge ordered. The four men laid the stretcher on the floor to the right of us. The judge leaned forward, peering down.

'Roman, why did you come here to murder?' he asked. I looked down at Tancinus. He raised his head, licked his lips, but said nothing.

'Roman, answer me!' the judge insisted, irritation in his voice.

'I, I do not understand,' Tancinus croaked in Latin.

'He has no Punic, your honour. I interviewed him last night,' the prosecutor interjected. The judge let out a heavy sigh.

'Then come over here, Hysux, and translate for me. I will not use in Carthage the language of Rome.'

The prosecutor crossed the room in front of us, before the bar. As he passed me, I smelled his sweat under the perfume of attar that he wore.

'Quintus Vitellius Tancinus,' Hysux asked in competent but accented Latin, 'Why did you come here to murder?'

'Someone sent me.'

'Who?'

'I cannot say,' Tancinus rasped.

'Who?'

'I repeat. I cannot say.'

The prosecutor Hysux walked forward to the bar, and translated for the judge, who replied: 'It does not matter. The facts are clear, as is the sentence. Death by decapitation. Take him away.'

'Your honour!' I was astonished. It was Bostar speaking.

'You wish to say something?' the judge replied, the clerks scribbling the words down.

'I do.'

'That is your right. Carry on.'

'Under your laws, the assailed can have all charges dismissed, is that not so?'

'It is.'

'Then I wish to have this man Tancinus set free.'

'Bost—' I exclaimed.

Looking at me with a wink, he put a finger to his lips for silence.

'Let me make sure I understand you. This Roman came to Carthage to murder you,' the judge continued with an edge to his voice, 'and yet you wish him pardoned.'

'That is the case, your honour.'

The judge sat back, and sighed deeply.

'Very well, then.' I saw him raise his eyebrows, and his brow furrow like desert sands. 'Let the records show this Tancinus as set free on the wish of the assailed. Like anyone who comes in peace to Carthage, the Roman may come freely here, and freely go. But, Hysux.'

'Your honour?'

'Tell this Roman that if he breaks a single law, if he so much as urinates in the street, I will have him flogged and expelled.' Tancinus beside us broke into a paroxysm of coughing. When he stopped, the judge went on: 'If, that is, he lives. Case dismissed. Keeper, stop the clock.'

*Document I found in a cache of Cato's private papers,
in a hidden recess under the floor of what used to be
his Senate room*

I write this for myself. I can have no other confessor, and I am
wracked with doubt about doing what, I know, must now be
done. Why am I the only one who understands the figures? My
fellow senators are all, without exception and unlike me, men of
great inherited wealth. Is this why they cannot see that Rome needs
money as a body blood? We must reform the corn supply. We must
replace our main aqueduct, and build another to the new blocks
of *insulae* beyond the Quirinal. Driven from their farms by slave
labour and the practices of the new estates my esteemed colleagues
run, at least 500 new people arrive in Rome each week. We need
them as smiths and soldiers, sailors, and I do all I can to encourage
them to come. Where do these immigrants find lodgings? Beyond
the Quirinal, where Flaccus' factors exact extortionate rents for
hovels and huts. What do they drink? Water from the marshes
of the Tiber, and they fall sick from rheums and fever. Soon, I
fear, there will be plague. We must build them a new aqueduct.
We must ensure adequate drains. Even in old Rome, the Cloaca
Maxima has not been attended to for over a hundred years. By
the forum Velabrum it is almost a stinking swamp. But of course
my colleagues cannot smell that from their villas high up on the
Palatine. These things having been done, we must rebuild Rome
– in stone. The poorer parts of the city, and that is most of it, are
of wood and mud and brick mixed with straw. The smallest fire
seems to burn down twenty homes. Stone. We must have stone.
And who has the finest quarries in the world? Carthage. *[This may
have been so. But there were and are many excellent quarries much*

closer to Rome. Cato's prejudice overwhelms his judgement. So do the irrational and rational conspire.]

I have been over and over our accounts with Marcus Antonius Regulus. He is a good and faithful servant of the Republic whom I should treat with more kindness. But I do not know how. This year, thanks largely to the war we are waging against Corinth, our expenditure will be almost a hundred thousand silver *denarii* over our income, and we debased the coinage with lead only a year ago. Yet if I raise this issue in the Senate, some wag remarks that net income and gross habits have always distinguished Rome, or something along those lines.

I raised myself from nothing. In the war against Hannibal, others fought in search of glory. They mocked me, Scipio in particular, but I stayed here in Rome. I worked night and day in the treasury and grain stores. I made sure there was iron for more *pila* points, wood for more arrows, bronze for more greaves when all in Rome said there was none. I commandeered bronze, for example, from the mint, and convinced the people that coinage of lead was sound. That is how Rome survived. I had stores of everything. I had planned. I fought that war as hard as anyone, day after day, from dusk to bleary dawn, not on a horse or shouting orders to conscripts but hour after hour, at a desk, poring over ledgers, I fought Hannibal in my mind. My election to the Censorship attests what I achieved. But let the gods at least bear witness: it was earned.

And now all we achieved is threatened once again. We need more income. That means more trade, and so more taxes. That means that Carthage is a wall that blocks our way. She controls, by the confounded treaty Scipio and others made after the last war, trading routes that Rome needs if she is to survive, let alone thrive. I am determined that we will wrest those routes from Carthage. That means she must die, and I must set certain matters in train. Hannibal's bastard has escaped me for the moment. But he may prove a cipher anyhow.

So why do I hesitate to move? Because my hatred of Carthage

scares me. It runs to depths I do not understand. And so let me try to write down that memory that engulfs me. Let me tell what I have never told. Perhaps that will free my weakened will.

I was twelve. I had run away from home, if that is what it can be called, from a so-called farm, a back-lying patch of stone and whin and milkthistle three miles from Tusculum. It was my father's compensation for losing his left arm in the first Punic War. But he knew how to use his right one. The brute beat me, often, daily, and my first memories are of pain and being scared. When I was cowed and cowering in a corner, he would beat my mother instead, and she bore her bruises as a badge of shame. I had two siblings, but their lives ended. My beatings did not.

So I went away. Hiding by day, walking by night, living on berries and stolen scraps I made my way to Ostia. Ship after ship refused the pleas of a bedraggled, malnourished, would-be cabin boy. I lived like a rat among the wharves and stays and tenders until, one autumn afternoon, a ship's master answered my prayers. The ship was called the *Tyrian*. That meant nothing to me. Nor did it that first evening when the captain told me in his broken Latin that they were Carthaginians, running iron ore to Sicily. Nothing but names. That has changed.

I was glad of the gruel they fed me that first night, and the tiny space up in the fo'c'sle among the spare sails that they said was my own. That first night only. The second night the captain came for me, ordered me to come down. Groggy, feeling seasick, I did as I was told. Suddenly, he pushed me down onto some old nets lying at the bottom of the hold. Pulling off his outer smock he lay down beside me, and began stroking my hair. Only when he moved his hands lower, tugging up my tattered tunic, did I begin to recognise the wrong. He sucked his right index finger, with its filthy, splintered nail and before I could think or move away it was in my anus and he groaned.

It was the pain, I think. My father had not hurt me there, but this Carthaginian was a man, causing me pain and I exploded, writhing, wriggling, flailing at him with my elbows and arms.

Panting, he rolled away from me, stood up, and smiled. 'What a little tiger we have here, then,' he said in Latin. Then he called out something in a language I couldn't understand and there were two more men beside him, winking, nodding at his words.

I crept back, back towards the ship's side. I smelt the salt, the oak, the caulk on pine. The two men, not the captain, pulled me by my legs towards them. There was only a little moonlight shining through the hatch of the hold. It was enough. I saw the mucus on the knob of the captain's swollen penis glistening in the light. I screamed, and screamed. They laughed, and laughed, and turned and held me, spreading out my legs, making me bend down. And then the captain buggered me, driving in and pulling out and driving in again, his calloused hands rasping at the cheeks of my bum.

I must have fainted. Then I was aware of lying on my belly on the net again. A different smell beside me, a different penis breaking in. Then I was flipped over, and I felt something in my mouth. I bit it, and felt only gladness for the darkness when the blow fell.

They left me in Sicily, in the harbour of Syracuse, a spent and broken shell. The captain had tired of me after two days, or was it four. Thereafter the whole crew of sixteen had taken their turn.

In Syracuse, I was lucky. A fisherman's widow, a toothless crone called Xanthippa, took pity on me and gave me room. The bleeding did not stop for days. From my early twenties, as soon as I could afford it, I sent Xanthippa money every year until I heard that she had died. Time has healed the wounds to my body, or almost: one of the reasons I have not been a soldier is that since that rape I have been unable to control my bowels. Defecation comes on me unannounced, and I can do nothing to hold it in. Before I enter the Senate, for example, first I always sit long on the latrine. But nothing, I think, will ever heal the wounds to my mind, or salve the hatred that burns in me for Carthage, and anyone of that blood.

I have never told anyone of this, not even Sempronia, my wife. I think I would disgust her if she knew. I think she would ask herself why I did not kill myself. Why didn't I? Writing this has helped me understand. I lived for revenge.

There is a strong and rational case for a third and final war against Carthage. But as in all these things, there are points for, and points against. On the one hand we could, for example, let Carthage be and seek instead to expand the Republic east, even beyond the Euxine Sea. On the other hand, there would be the danger that Carthage tried the same. The Senate would debate such things for days. I can save them the trouble. There is an objective case against Carthage anyway; and there is mine. My mind is set and clear. Carthage must be destroyed.

[I do not know whether to feel mirth or pity at this strange apology, which I have reproduced here in full. So buggery begat the final Punic War? I suppose there are stranger truths.

Anyway I do think it worth drawing attention to the last phrase of this document: 'Delenda est Carthago.' This is of interest to a mind like mine, because it is as far as I can ascertain Cato's earliest use of what became a famous phrase. He was to use it in innumerable speeches to the Senate, through most of which in the course of my researches I have read. Whatever the subject, be that the corn supply, or the coinage, or citizenship, Cato always managed to relate it to Carthage and end his speech with the phrase – in indirect speech, of course – 'Censeo etiam Delendam esse Carthaginem.' 'It is my firm opinion that Carthage must be destroyed.' I should not be surprised were this to become a commonplace of the grammarians and pedagogues.]

As for Scipio, I will watch and wait. He is miscegenated, whatever his name, whoever his father, however they nurture him, and so may be his nature. His father was corrupt. The son may be too. It is too early to tell, but this Scipio may not prove the threat that he seems. Meantime, there are certain things I can do – and will.

From Bostar's journal

I did a strange thing yesterday. A Roman called Quintus Vitellius Tancinus tried to kill me the day before. I have not asked him, but I do not need to. Cato sent him here. How did he find us? I have been foolhardy. Perhaps I have been eating too many dates. They lighten the mind. I must accelerate my plans. Anyway, as is my right under Carthaginian law I had Tancinus set free. He is in the city hospital, hovering between life and death from the wound Hanno gave him in my defence. Tomorrow we leave for Mastanabal's boar hunt, though I imagine we will be hunting more than boar. I should think we will be gone for three or four days. If he is still alive when we get back, I will make Tancinus an offer. I think he might find it an interesting one.

From Cato's papers

The widow Apurnia in Capua, to Hanno her son. We have heard from Labienus in Rome. He tells us that you are in Carthage, and safe. I pray that is not wrong. I thank the gods, but still I do not hear from you. Let me have news of you, my son. Artixes is writing this down for me, but the words strain. I only want to hold you in my arms. Are you eating well? I hope you have a warm cloak, now that winter has come.

Here the even temper of my life goes on. I see to my lodgers. I shop and cook and clean and think but rarely of what might have been. But I am ill at ease. Yesterday I witnessed an ugly scene in the market. Some Carthaginian jewellers had set up a stall – as they have every right to do. At least I assume they had paid their dues, or the police would not have let them trade. Anyway, as I was walking past their stall I heard a swarthy Capuan swear at them. 'Bloody Poeni,' he said. 'You're not welcome here!' Soon, others joined him and they began chanting 'Poeni, home! Poeni home!' It turned quite nasty. I felt violence in the air.

Why is it always thus with men? I hope you will be one of peace, not war. I often think of the many souls your father is responsible for, and hope that he is not tormented but knows the peace I felt him crave when he was with me, when he was in me, when we made you – Artixes has raised an eyebrow. Yes, the market. Well, the police came, and quietened things down. But I have a strange sense the incident was orchestrated. I saw two men, strangers, standing at the top of the lane, watching. As soon as the police came, they were gone. Tell me if you do not think that odd. Or perhaps it is mere imagining. Write to me, Hanno. Write. Your loving mother.

From Bostar's journal

I had never seen such fine silk before. I touched the curtains of the litter that called for us at daybreak. It felt softer than young skin. I wonder where the Carthaginians find such stuff as this? Preceded by a steward on foot, six slaves carried Hanno and me, rolling and richly caparisoned, Hanno still rubbing sleep from his eyes. Where we were going, I did not know. But towards breakfast, I hoped. I remembered I had forgotten to bring gum.

The litter stopped, was lowered down, the curtain opened. I stepped out first, into a strengthening sun that slanted across the sand and stuccoed walls of a wide courtyard I knew: that of the temple of Eschmoun. In a corner of the yard, I saw a fine pavilion of embroidered cotton cloth, and emerging from that towards us walked Astylax.

'Good morning, Bostar of Chalcedon,' he called.

'And the same to you,' I replied. As he came close, he bowed. Unlike Romans, Carthaginians do not touch to greet. Fear of disease, perhaps, or dirt prevents them, or ancient memory of some old taboo. I returned the compliment, and said: 'Astylax, this is Hanno, my charge.'

This time he did not bow, but peered intently at Hanno. 'Indeed,' he said after a pause. 'Hanno Barca, we are led to believe. Well, the High Sufet awaits you. Follow me. You must be hungry.'

In a tunic and trousers, with boots of brushed kidskin up to his knees, we found Mastanabal in the pavilion, standing plate in hand beside a sheeted trestle table which groaned with food. At one end of it were dishes of hot fare, kept warm by little oil burners, then silver salvers of bread and rolls, golden ones with cheeses, and bowls and bowls of fruit – quinces, pomegranates, bergamots, apples, figs and, I was pleased to see despite myself, delicious-looking dates.

The Sufet turned. 'Welcome, Bostar,' he piped. 'And this,' his voice slowing, 'must be Hanno.'

To his credit, Hanno stepped forward. 'I am, Lord Sufet,' he said. 'Hanno – Barca.'

The pause was almost imperceptible, but it was there. My senses sharpened. I saw that I must pick my way with care. Mastanabal, I thought, stiffened. But all he said, looking Hanno up and down, was: 'Indeed, indeed.' Then, changing tone, he went on: 'Now, come and join me in these small trifles. The kitchen steward says the quails' eggs are particularly good. Eat well. A long journey awaits us. Oh, Astylax,' the Sufet said, looking round for him, 'before we begin I presume that you have tasted all these dishes?'

Astylax stepped forwards, bowed and raised his head. 'I have, my Lord – except for the eggs. As you see, they are unshelled.'

'Good, Astylax, good,' Mastanabal replied.

'"Tasted", my Lord Sufet?' I enquired, surprised.

'Against poison, Bostar of Chalcedon,' he said mildly. 'You see Astylax is more than my secretary. He is my bulwark and my shield.'

'But who would—' Hanno interjected.

Astylax cut him off. 'Rome's assassins are everywhere,' he said with what I thought was a strange smile. 'You of all people should know that, Hanno.'

Letter found among papers in the citadel of Carthage

Cato the Censor to Astylax in Carthage. Never write to me directly of these matters. Inform me immediately, but obliquely, if the third of Bostar's proposals you told me of comes to be. That would be a straightforward violation of the treaty. That would be, alone, *casus belli.*

Letter preserved in the archives of Neapolis

Titus Licinius Labienus to Rufus Curtius Flaminius. I have returned safely to Rome. Your man Demodocus' horses were as sound on the way back as they were when I came. One filly bucked and threw me when a sudden storm of lightning struck and scared her, but I escaped with only a bad bruise to my left knee. Thank you for your hospitality. Your gardens are a particular delight. You work miracles with that thin, volcanic soil. And now you are no longer a senator, as you said you will have even more time to devote to that pursuit. I will as promised write today to Artixes in Capua and have him send you some cuttings from my jacaranda tree.

I find Scipio well. His Latin has improved a great deal in the ten days I have been away. I have yet to meet Ennius, but your recommendation was clearly a good one. Even so, I think it is too early for me to begin telling him what we agreed. As for his two other tutors, I have yet to receive a report. But Theogenes is joining me for dinner tonight, and I will no doubt learn more then. Oh, we are being watched here. They must be Cato's men. But that will come as no surprise.

From Bostar's journal

Hanno and I sat on a bench opposite Mastanabal at a long table of cedar wood. In what I felt to be a strained silence we ate our breakfast, washed down with a delicious cordial of lime. I resisted the dates after all. When we had finished, the Sufet clapped his hands. Four servant girls in bright green robes came from behind a silken screen and cleared our plates away. Hanno kept darting glances at one of them, a pretty, lithe girl with dancing eyes and lustrous, curling hair but with a long scar right across her left cheek.

Mastanabal, of course, noticed. He notices everything through those often half-shut eyes. 'Do you two know each other?' he asked Hanno, before staring at the girl. She blushed. Hanno looked confused.

'No. Well, yes – in a manner of speaking that is. I mean that I have seen her before,' he said.

'Oh, and where might that have been?' the Sufet enquired, clearly amused.

'In the market, just after they arrived,' the girl gave back with I thought considerable pluck for someone in her station.

'Quiet, girl!' Astylax barked. 'You know you are not to speak unless—'

'That's all right, Astylax,' Mastanabal interrupted, turning on him a winning smile. 'You are right to uphold the proprieties. But tell me, girl,' he went on, his attention changing to her, 'what is your name?'

'Fetopa, my Lord Sufet,' eyes averted, she replied.

'And a very fine—'

Just then, the trumpeting of an elephant filled the air *[this is a* deus ex machina *worthy of Euripides.]* and then another, then a third. I closed my eyes, remembering the last time I had heard that noise in a different place, a different world. I shook the memory away. I opened my eyes.

Mastanabal was wiping his thin lips, so small for the rest of him, with a napkin. As the noise subsided, he stood up, saying: 'Good. Perfect timing. Gentlemen, are you ready? As you may have gathered, our elephants are here.'

Outside, in the courtyard, ears flapping, trunks swaying, tails swishing, ten of them stood in a row. Each had a howdah on its back, covered with velvets and silks secured by a wide girth. As one, the elephants moved towards us, and stopped four strides away. I glanced at Hanno. Licking his lips and playing with his hair, he was looking nervous until his face brightened. 'Look, Bostar!' he blurted. 'It's Halax!'

From behind the line of elephants, a boy, a man, I could not tell, walked or rather scuttled towards us, bearing the biggest hunchback I have ever seen. He ignored us, and stopped in front of Mastanabal. 'Good morning, Sufet,' he said with easy familiarity in a strange, high-pitched voice that sang as he craned his eyes up. 'I thought you could ride Asta today.'

'Thank you, Halax,' Mastanabal replied. 'But I will ride with our friend Bostar here. I believe you have a double howdah fitted on one of your charges?'

'I do, my Lord. On Xasa, the old bull over there.' He pointed, and I noticed his strangely fine fingers, to the last elephant in the line.

'Yes, yes. Xasa. We meet again.' The Sufet and Halax exchanged a strange glance. 'Good. Bostar, you will ride with me. Hanno, with Halax. You know each other, I believe.'

'We do, my Lord, we do,' Hanno replied confidently.

Mahouts appeared. Slaves brought ladders. I followed Mastanabal's ponderous buttocks up, adjusted my cushions, sat down and we were on our way.

Letter preserved in the archives of Rome

Cato to Ennius. I understand you are acting as tutor to Scipio. I write to express my disappointment, and discontent. Did I not bring you to Rome, support and encourage you, secure you the commission to write a history of our Republic to this day? I ask you, resign from this post, at once.

Letter found among Cato's papers [written, I might add, in a most elegant hand]

Ennius to Marcus Porcius Cato, Censor of Rome. I have yours of this morning. I shall of course be always in your debt. But I have been faithful all my life to the cause of learning. This young man drinks in what I have to teach him like parched ground. I care nothing for his name. He is a student, I a teacher. So even at the risk of incurring your displeasure, I will continue what I have begun. When Scipio ceases to want to learn, I will cease to teach.

From Hanno's memoir

I had never been in the countryside before. Yes, I had seen the fields outside Capua, and the forests of Macedonia. But the land outside Carthage stretched as far as the eye could see. The Sufet's guard marching behind us, we swayed in single file through the salt marshes landward of the city, through the clamour of cranes, of jabirus and jacanas jostling to move out of our way. It was a halcyon autumn day, the air crisp and clear, the sky cloudless and cerulean blue, the wind warm from the west.

We entered grassland, where cattle and sheep grazed, tended by boys and girls who stared impassively at us as we passed. 'Where are we going, Halax?' I asked him, squeezed on the single seat beside me.

'To the Sufet's lodge, a morning's ride away in the forests south-west of here.'

'Have you been there before?'

'Often. As far as I know, Mastanabal never goes without me.'

'That seems strange.'

'What does?'

'This relationship between you, a potter's son and a—'

'Go on. Say it. A hunchback.'

I felt myself blush, saw the anger in his eyes.

'Between you and the High Sufet of Carthage,' I went on softly.

'It isn't strange at all,' Halax replied, brightening. 'He's my friend.'

'How did that come to be?'

'Simple. Elephants, of course. Well, one in particular,' he said with a smile. 'That one,' and he pointed to the bull bearing Bostar and Mastanabal ahead of us.

'Really? Tell me.'

'I love elephants. You know that. But you don't know why. When I was born, Hanno, they put me in the bull elephants' stable, you know the one in the wall, to be trampled to death. That's what we do with children born deformed.'

'But that's murder!'

'Perhaps. But that's the way here. Anyway, when my mother came back the next morning – illegally, I might add – to collect my corpse, I was alive. The elephants hadn't hurt me in any way. On the contrary, my mother said, she found me being licked by one of them. She took it as a sign from Eschmoun and reared me secretly, hiding me from the *mehashebim*. That's why she works at the front of our house, not in the backyard—'

'I see. So no one would walk through your house.'

'Exactly. Are you thirsty, by the way? There should be a water skin under the seat.'

'No, thanks. I'm fine. Carry on with your story, please.'

'As early as I can remember, I dreamed of elephants. As I grew, I used to visit them in the walls.'

'Wasn't that dangerous? Someone might have seen you.'

'I suppose so. But I was very careful. I used to go at night, and slip in.'

'That's how you learned to talk to them?'

'Yes. Well, they talked to me. I copied their sounds.'

'But how did you become a friend of the Sufet?'

'I was coming to that. It was ten years ago. He was being carried in a litter along the street that passes our house. The other side of the street to ours had been cleared to build new houses – it had been a timber yard. There were elephants working on the site, moving rubble and stone. I used to sit all day and watch them through our kitchen window. There were three cows, and a bull, and the smallest cow was going lame. I think she had torn a nail. They have three nails on their hind feet, you know, and five on the front. But their keeper didn't notice the lame cow, or if he did, he didn't care. They have incredibly sensitive feet, elephants, you know. I have seen them stand on a turtle, but feel it and lift the foot away, leaving the turtle unharmed.'

I squeezed Halax's arm, and smiled. 'Halax, Halax!' I laughed gently. 'The Sufet!'

Halax chuckled. 'Oh, yes. It's simple. The bull went berserk.'

'Berserk? What does that mean?'

'It means they go mad. They lose control.'

'But why?'

'Who knows? What makes people lose their temper? I should think the keeper had been mistreating him. He had welts on his ears. Anyway, this bull – that's him, by the way, Xasa, up ahead, just went berserk and came charging down the street. I thought he was going to run straight into our wall.'

'But he didn't?'

'No. He caught sight of the Sufet's litter, I suppose it was the bright colours. I saw him hit it with his head, and it soared up into the air. The bearers ran for their lives. The litter landed, and Xasa was bashing it with his trunk and rearing for the trample when I got there.'

'You showed yourself?'

'Of course. I didn't think.'

'And what did you do?'

'Oh, I just called out to Xasa. Told him to stop, and then got between him and the litter and reached up and tugged his ears.'

In front of us, Xasa stopped suddenly. His mahout lowered the ladder, and Bostar began climbing down. 'Sorry,' he called out to us. 'Too much of that lime cordial!' I waved at him, and turned back to Halax.

'And that was that?'

'Almost. The Sufet emerged from his litter, bruised but unharmed. He told me he was very grateful, and I introduced him to my mother. He offered her a reward for my saving his life. She said we lacked for nothing. What about your husband, he asked. He died at Zama, she replied. By this time surrounded by fussing *mehashebim* and retainers, I am sorry, the Sufet answered, and

I knew he meant it. There is something you could do for me, Lord Sufet, I said. And what is that, he asked. Make me keeper of the city's elephants. They are my friends. He agreed.

By this time Bostar had regained his seat. 'And that, Hanno,' Halax concluded, 'is what I have been to this day. For saving the life of the Sufet, I have been Carthage's only hunchback, and its elephants' keeper and friend.'

Letter preserved in the archives of Rome

Labienus to Theogenes in Vicenza. My dear friend, I know you are away on business, but I would be grateful for your advice. In the months Scipio has been here, he has grown in confidence, assuredness, culture and prowess at arms. It may well be that he becomes the man strong enough to withstand Cato and his party, and ensure peace with Carthage, not war. Already people flock to him in the Forum, reminding him of his father's fame.

But there are traits in him I do not like at all. Yesterday I caught him at it again, rutting with a slave girl in the kitchen of all places, indeed on the floor. He cannot, it seems, see a woman but he must have her. I doubt there is a female in your house here under forty and over twelve he has not slept with. I am fearful of pregnancies and scandal, yes, but of something more.

This morning the housekeeper Ayla asked to see me. The girl whose ravishing I interrupted had complained to her – about force. It seems that Scipio does not use his charm alone. The girl told Ayla that he had been pestering her for weeks, and she resisting his advances. Yesterday the other slaves were in the baths for delousing and he followed her into the kitchen, drew a knife on her and told her to lie down there and then. Having sent her away to the slave market immediately, of course, I cannot question the girl myself. Anyway Scipio would deny her charge, and call her a lying cow.

Men's libido, and women's too, is I know as different as their faces. But Scipio must learn some self control. He must also learn respect for people. Are we not, whatever our station, equal before the gods and the law? I will not endure his treating women, whether slave or free, as mere objects for his gratification.

So, advise me on this old friend, as you would have advised the father of the son. Secondly, Scipio has proposed that, being now of age, he moves into his father's villa as of the festival of the Saturnalia. He will then be free, as you know, to spend his wealth as he pleases. I fear the worst. What, if anything, can or should we do?

Letter preserved in the archives of Rome

Cato the Censor to Spurius Lingustus. Your reports have been excellent. Well done. They have served to confirm what I already knew, namely the allies, friends, clients and confederates of this new Scipio. Like father, like son. But that is as well. At least I know where I stand, and I would say the parties as represented in the Senate are evenly drawn.

You may now pay off your men. Abandon your watch on the villa of Curtius. Come and see me as soon as you can.

Letter preserved in the archives of Rome

I am terrified, and risk my life by setting this down. But, my dear wife Silvia, I must tell someone – not that there is anything I can do – and I know the next courier on the list. He is a half-wit, who can neither read nor write, but he is faithful and I know that this will reach you. There is someone called Spurius Lingustus, an 'associate' of Cato's. At least that is what he calls them. He was a centurion. He is a big man, and has always frightened me. He came to Cato's rooms this morning, here in the Senate. I know I should not have, but I listened at the door. I caught most of it. There is an important fleet leaving Ostia just after the next full moon. I know. Cato himself arranged it. Three merchantmen, protected by one galley of war, will be taking gold and papers and essential supplies to our new colony at Dyrrhacium. This Lingustus is to travel at all speed to Rhodes. You will know of that den of vipers. There he is to employ three pirate ships, who are to attack and sink all but one of our four vessels – the survivor, of course, to bear the news to Rome that their attackers were Carthaginian. Yes, the pirates are to fly Carthaginian flags and speak only in Punic, which should not be hard since half of those scoundrels are Carthaginian anyway.

[I omit what follows: maudlin self-pity, and fears. Still, Speusippus' position cannot have been an easy one.]

From Hanno's memoir

Half the Sufet's Guard were now in front, and half behind. Having climbed for miles, now the track wound down, so twisting that, time after time, we moved on back into our own dust. I saw movement in the trees. Heads. Legs. Horses?

'Look, Halax,' I said, pointing, 'what are those?'

He followed my arm. 'Oh, onagers – wild asses. And very tasty they are too. Mastanabal usually has one while he is here. But over there! Can you see it? There is a muntjac, a small deer. They are very shy – and rare.'

We rounded another bend. Through the trees I saw a sinuous, green river winding through a verdant valley. Our elephant raised its trunk, trumpeted and quickened its pace. Halax chirped some strange noises, and it slowed. 'It is the river,' he said.

'Can they see that far?' I asked.

'No. But they can smell.'

I was hungry. I looked at Halax, who smiled at me. 'You hungry too? Don't worry, we'll soon be there.'

The Sufet's lodge was one huge, single storey by the river, everything, even the roof tiles, made of wood. We were expected. As the elephants bathed and sprayed and wallowed in the river, on the house's terrace we had lunch of golden pheasant, cooked over seasoned cherry wood and sprinkled with marjoram. We had not quite finished when it began.

Breaking the deep silence, drowning the river's tintinabulation, from the forested hilltops ringing us a searing ululation came. My jaw dropped. I looked around, and back at Mastanabal, who smiled.

'No need to be alarmed, young man. That will be Massinissa, and his men.'

'Massinissa?' Bostar interjected. 'That is a Numidian name.'

'Close,' Mastanabal replied. 'Well done. But it is a Libyic name. Numidians have no "m", but use "vh" instead. Massinissa has a cousin called Vhassinissa, for example.'

The sound above us stopped as suddenly as it had begun. The Sufet stretched out his arms, and yawned. 'Let Astylax explain.'

Sitting opposite me, next to Mastanabal, Astylax did as he was bidden. 'This is Libyican land.'

'Not Carthaginian?' I asked.

Astylax laughed. 'Patience, patience, please!' Beside me, Bostar placed a gentle hand on my left knee. 'The Libyicans are our allies, and Massinissa is their king. His rule extends into the desert west and south of here. They safeguard our caravans—'

'For, of course, a fee,' Mastanabal chipped in. 'They are also the best hunters in the world, as you will see. Why, here they are!'

I could see horsemen, perhaps two hundred, most wearing white and all in strange headgear, emerge from the trees. They kicked their mounts on as the land levelled towards the river. They bunched towards the ford that we had crossed and raced towards us. By the time we had stood up, it seemed, they were there on the grass below us, their horses snorting and jostling as the men dismounted with a practised ease.

They were all black. Well, almost. Some were nearer to charcoal, but all had low foreheads and wide, splayed noses and lips that were full and red. One of them – he had the finest teeth that I have ever seen – stepped forward.

'So, Lord Sufet, welcome!' he exclaimed. The words were Punic, but the accent quite its own.

'Thank you, Massinissa. As always, it is a great pleasure to be here,' Mastanabal replied. 'Now, you know Astylax of course.' The King of the Libyicans nodded. The Sufet went on. 'But you do not know our two guests, Bostar of Chalcedon, and Hanno – Barca,' he said evenly, gesturing at us in turn. What was going on? Was Mastanabal acknowledging me? If so, why?

The King stepped forward. Only the rail of the terrace was between us. He had large, round, black and penetrating eyes.'Barca?' he asked me, 'Barca?' in his deep and rumbling voice. 'Who was your father?'

I squared round to face him. 'My father, King Massinissa,' I said clearly, 'was Hannibal.'

The men behind him ceased to fidget. I felt their interest as a wave. In one movement, Massinissa vaulted onto the terrace and stood, a head taller than me, shutting out the sun. I smelled his sweat. I felt his hand, strong on my right arm. I did not know what was going on. But I was not afraid.

Massinissa stepped back, reached out his arms to hold me by my shoulders. I looked up at him. He had a boil on his chin. His breath was foul. 'Hanno,' he said. 'Your father, and his father, were my friends.' With that, he embraced me, and behind us his men cheered.

As Massinissa released me, Mastanabal moved back from the table and spoke out. 'Now then, Massinissa, shall we see if these hills hold any boar? Hanno, can you use a bow and arrow, or a spear?'

'No, Lord Sufet,' I replied. 'I have never learned.'

'Well, it's time you did,' he gave me back, 'and that time is now.'

Letter preserved in the archives of Neapolis

It was a dramatic entrance, my old friend. Regulus himself, Admiral of the Eastern Fleet, bursting into the Curia. I do not know what is going on, Curtius, but I do not like it. In short, our ships bound for Dyrrhacium have been attacked, and most of them sunk, by Carthaginians. Regulus was in no doubt. On behalf of the Senate Pulcher has just written to Mastanabal in Carthage for an explanation. Whatever he says, it had better be good. I need you. Now that Scipio has left your villa for his father's, now his own, would you not return to Rome? For a time at least, until we see which way the wind blows? At the moment, I fear it is ill. Give me your answer, by return. Flaccus.

From Bostar's journal

We returned this afternoon from the country and the boar hunt.
Hanno acquitted himself well. But the most fruitful parts of the
experience were the rides there and back on an elephant which
Mastanabal and I shared. He fenced with me, he explored. And
then he plunged. He gave, he took away.

Hanno is now to be recognised by the Council of Carthage as
his father's heir. But he must first survive something known as the
Passage of Ordeal. I do not know what that means, but it gives
me fear. I am to speak to one Gulussa, High Priest, about it. All
Mastanabal would tell me is that I must get Hanno fit for it: 'very,
very fit', he urged, 'his body, I mean. His mind you cannot prepare.'
Well, I will find a trainer tomorrow morning. Apparently there is a
Spartan, a mercenary soldier, who excels at such things. He runs
some kind of school.

So I am progressing towards my first objective. It has cost a great
deal, but that is what the money is for. I am to finance a trading
expedition in Mastanabal's name. It seems his family, as is the way
in Carthage, have held for generations the monopoly on trading
topaz. The Barcas' right, incidentally, is to murex. They own all
the coastal fisheries for it, but these were ruined in the last war
and will need much, Mastanabal told me, to restore. I will go and
see for myself. It seems I am to become a merchant once again.

First, though, there is the Sufet's topaz. The mines are in Senegalia,
a three-month caravan from here. I am to buy Mastanabal two
hundred camels, equipment and provisions, and have drivers hired.
Africanus would be amused.

My second objective, if I can trust Mastanabal, is achieved. He
will order the secret construction – with my money – of three

hundred new galleys of war. They will be built in four separate, secluded shipyards down the coast near Clupea and Leptis. Mastanabal assures me that under the treaty, and I think I can detect Africanus' hand here, the Romans have rights of inspection only in the shipyards of Carthage. They will remain still.

Finally, peace, a peace of equals. The house of Scipio, the staff of Rome, has a representative again. But how is he developing? He is young enough, as Cato and the other warmongers age, to assume dominance; he is unformed enough to absorb what Labienus and others teach him. But which way will he turn? He could be, like his uncle, a nonentity. He could be, like many, something much worse. *[Perhaps I have misjudged Bostar. Perhaps he is an optimist, rather than naïve.]* I wish I could go and judge for myself. But somehow, I do not think I would be allowed to return. Perhaps it was seeing boars speared, caught in a circle of men, but I am conscious of my own mortality; I sense my certitude failing, as in this month of November – *Yerach*, they call it here – the light lessens, and we feel the coming of cold.

Letter preserved in the archives of Neapolis

Lucius Valerius Flaccus to Rufus Curtius Flaminius. It did not turn out, I am afraid, as we might have hoped. The Senate was packed, a full house, and he had as many friends there as Cato. But Scipio, I am concluding with reluctance, is not half the man his father was. This first visit to the Curia by a young patrician is a time for solemnity and respect. I am sure you remember yours. The speech you are invited to give has one, simple *locus*: the *memoria* of your family, what they gave to Rome and the contribution you would like to make were the honour of a seat on these benches ever yours.

I am sure Scipio had been instructed well by Labienus and others. Indeed, in that I played some small part. But as he stood before the house there was an arrogance, a certain insouciance about him that does not augur well. For a start, he had not tied his hair back. He has a great deal of fine hair, a wavy brown. He kept his hands behind his back when, as you know, from respect and in humility they should have been by his sides. And so on.

As for what he said, it was rote learning, like the parrot at Macro's, the barber that I use. And his Latin is still far from good. At this rate, perhaps it never will be. Anyway, there were titters from Cato's party at several of his solecisms. The whole thing was not a success. I judge Scipio to have made no new enemies, certainly. But then nor has he won new friends, while his shameless wooing of the common people is not something for which we had planned.

Do you remember our old friend Gallus Celer, and that tiger he brought back to Rome from the Syrian war? He tried to civilise it, but it maimed one keeper after another. The city Guard had to kill it in the end.

Meanwhile, old friend, my head is full of numbers. Our siege of Corinth is not going well. Marcellus, our commander there, has asked us for more men and munitions. I am seeing the Treasury tomorrow to see what can be done. Fortunately, Cato is coming with me. He has his uses, you know.

From Bostar's journal

'So, Tancinus, you are going to live,' I said.

'Looks like it,' he grunted back from his bed.

'And then what?'

'Get out of here.'

'Oh, really? For where?'

His face fell. He raised his head and, wincing, looked at me. 'You don't have to rub it in, Bostar,' he said. 'I've got a wife back in Rome, and a child.'

'Then go back to them.'

'Sure. I wouldn't get as far as the end of the docks. You know that.' He fell back.

I felt pity for him. 'I don't know it, but I think it highly unlikely that Cato would let you live.'

He closed his eyes. I sat down on a chair beside his bed. In the next bed, a young child called out in fever. A nurse came.

'Cato? You knew?' Tancinus said quietly, opening his eyes and looking at the ceiling where flies buzzed.

'Of course. Who else?'

He turned to look at me. 'You were a friend of Africanus', weren't you?'

'I was.'

'A great man. Saved us from Hannibal, almost on his own. My brother fought under him. Said he was a genius, not a general. Never did understand why Cato hated him.' Pushing a trolley, the water boy approached. Tancinus waved him away. 'So what do you want, then?' he continued after a pause.

'I have an offer for you.'

'Oh yes. What's that then? A duel?'

'No, Tancinus. Save your sarcasm. I am not a fighting man. I want to offer you a job.'

This time, he sat right up, throwing back his blanket. I saw the dressing on his side. 'When, that is,' I went on, 'you're fully recovered.'

He stared at me. 'Look, I tried to kill you.'

'No,' I answered. 'Not me. What you were told I was. An enemy of Rome. Which, I might add, is one thing I am not. So, will you work for me?'

'Doing what, exactly?'

'This and that. But no killing. At least not any I have planned.'

'What, then?'

'You were a soldier, yes?'

'I was, for sixteen years. A *primus pilus*, then a centurion by the end,' he said proudly.

'Where did you serve?'

'All over. But Sicily, mostly.'

'And you took part in the siege of Syracuse?'

'How did you know that?'

'I didn't. I just hoped you had.'

'Because?'

'Tancinus, do you think you could help me prepare Carthage for a siege?'

He laughed. 'A siege, of Carthage! Anyone who tried would have to be mad. You've seen the walls, the harbour—'

'Mad, yes,' I replied. 'Or very, very determined. But answer me: could you help?'

He scratched his growing beard. 'First time I shaved, you know. Just before our final attack on Syracuse, once we'd breached the walls. Metellus, he was our general, and a fine soldier, said it would be fierce in there, fighting hand to hand. So he ordered all beards off, so the enemy would have less to grab.'

'Interesting. But my question?'

'What about my wife and daughter? They'll starve. I have to get back to them, somehow.'

'Or—' I began.

'Or what?'

'Or, easier, we could bring them to you here.'

After a moment, he began to laugh and then, pressing a hand to his wound, he doubled over in pain. He slowed his panting, and held up his head. 'Don't make me laugh, please.'

'Is that a "no"?'

'Come back tomorrow. I'll give you my answer then.'

I did. He agreed.

Letter preserved in the citadel of Carthage

Claudius Metellus Pulcher, Senator and Consul of Rome, to Mastanabal, High Sufet, and the Council of Carthage. My colleagues have elected me to speak for them on this issue. Your recent attack on our shipping is a flagrant violation of the treaty between us. We lost three merchantmen at your pirates' hands. We want: (1) compensation for this, to the amount of 10,000 gold *denarii* or its equivalent and five hundred *heminae* of wheat; (2) your personal assurance that this act was one of your pirates', and not condoned by the state; (3) a member of your nobility to come here to Rome, hostage as surety that such a thing will not occur again. Give your reply to him who brings this. If we do not have that, and a satisfactory one, within seven days of writing, we will begin to sink all Carthaginian shipping we find. Any retaliation to that, we will proclaim as *casus belli*.

Letter preserved in the archives of Rome

Cato to Flaccus. I suspect that I might as well save the Treasury the cost of this parchment. But I wish to protest formally about the advancement of Scipio. He is not advancing up the *cursus honorum*. He simply treats it as his own. And he breaks, flagrantly, all our sumptuary laws. Will you allow this to go on?

Letter preserved among Cato's papers

Flaccus to Cato. I am using, as you can see, only the very smallest piece of parchment. That is because my answer to you is short: yes.

[Scipio told me only late last night. We leave Rome at dusk. We are going away, to Corinth. Lucius Mummius Achaicus, who is Scipio's cousin and proconsul of the Roman legions there, has asked specifically for Scipio as an expert on sieges, and me as an adviser. So, another city, another sack.

I must hurry. Much of the material that ends my mosaic is already in order. But editing what covers the events in between will take a great deal of time, and that I do not have. After Corinth, I am to accompany the Roman fleet in search of the Cassiterides, those misty islands to the west from which Carthage long drew its tin and silver, and much of its wealth, whatever treaties said. The route to them is one thing Cato was never able to ascertain, and I discovered among the papers I found after Carthage's extirpation. I look forward to the Atlantic. They say that, beyond the Pillars of Herakles (yes, I insist on the Greek form of his name), the sea is no longer blue, but black. We shall see.

When I come back, I have my own history to finish. So I must deal with this dalliance today. That is a pity, but one which I cannot gainsay. And, who knows? It may suit the tenor of these times when little is finished, but much begun. So, with the aid of two scribes – both Greek of course, for Roman letters are still but rude, whatever Ennius might argue – I will abbreviate my selection of documents, and accelerate the passage of time. Then I will dictate a synopsis of what remains of this telling tale I hoped would tell its own. I will leave the scribes to bind the whole together. That is fitting. Life too is the work of many hands. Like the chorus, one man may lead. But many play.]

Letter preserved in the archives of Rome

Theogenes in Vicenza to Labienus in Rome. Forgive my delayed response to yours. I have been travelling in the hills around here. The silver filigree is very good, and I have purchased several fine screens. Your news of Scipio concerns me – although it would not, were he of any other name. Unlike you Romans, we Greeks have never had any form of inheritance tax. We know from long experience that families always tax themselves in the end. The lineage of the Scipios is long and, for the most part, illustrious. It was time they had a wastrel to disgrace them, and empty their coffers so that, with someone else, somewhere else, the cycle could begin again.

But on this occasion, if we can we must subvert the natural order. I see matters as a game of chess. One side has Cato. We too need a king, even if his knights and castles direct him, and Scipio is our man. With his name behind us, the People would never let Cato and the Senate enact measures of which we do not approve. Let me be clear, especially given the rumours I have heard, even here. I do not want war with Carthage. It is damn bad for my business, and my pleasure. In the last war, it was impossible to procure Falernian wine, and who wanted to buy art when they were riding to kill or be killed?

Scipio is young for a start. And think of your beloved garden in Capua – which, I might add, you must be missing. As you know, transplants often take time to root and thrive. So, I have a solution. Put it to Curtius. It should ensure that Scipio calms down, and will allow you time to return home. Send Scipio off to an army somewhere. You know I do not follow these things, but there is always trouble somewhere on our frontiers. Gaul, for example.

There is always some tribe no one has heard of chopping off an obscure procurator's head, or raping his wife, and all that sort of thing. Find out. Then, as a tribune perhaps, nothing too fancy, a praetor would be going too far, send Scipio there. If he fornicates with Gauls, you know what will happen. Let us let it. There's nothing like a good dose of the pox to calm a young stud down.

Letter preserved in the citadel of Carthage

Bodmelqart to Mastanabal, High Sufet of Carthage. I have done as you bid me. Hugging first our coast, we came to the Pillars of Hirqalexh and crossed to Spain. By day we moored in creeks and sheltered bays. We sailed only by night, keeping closely to the coast, and I am sure neither Roman nor any man that breathes has seen us. I write this moored off the town the Romans now call Emporiae, that was Qatash when it was a Punic place. May it be so again. Because of what I have seen I am sending one of our two ships back with this letter, so that you may give me word.

As you ordered, alone I journeyed inland. I found Fanar, the place we first discovered just before the last war. Your misgivings are sound. The Roman insistence that the veins of silver we had found there were shallow and worthless is, as you suspected, false. The Romans have dug great mines. I saw four. Though I did not go close, I marked many slaves go down. So something we ceded for nothing under the treaty is worth an incalculable amount.

Might the same be true of the claims that we forewent, under the selfsame shaming treaty, north-north-west of Narabo? The journey would be perilous. The western Roman fleet has a station hard by, and Narabo itself is a lee shore. I would like to go, but await your instructions. Shall I seek more proof of the duplicity of Rome?

From Bostar's journal

I am exhausted. It is barely dawn, and I am writing this by candle-light. I was with the Council until nearly midnight, but could not sleep when I returned. Borage. I must get the cook to prepare tea of borage. And ask her to find a fuller. Now it is spring, our latrine smells, and harbours flies. It must be full.

I would ask Hanno to go and find a fuller now. This is the time of day they clean the city's drains. But I am sure that he is still sleeping. He should be, given the rigours of his training school.

I was summoned without warning. Hanno and I were eating, but I left without delay. I found myself in a full meeting of the Council. The hall was huge, the members sitting in carved, high-backed chairs around its walls, but the acoustic was good. I could not understand the proto-Punic of the prayers and imprecations. What I do understand is the letter which a fat sweating steward, a eunuch, I would guess, gave me to read as that was going on.

Then I was escorted to the middle of the room, and a stool brought. It was made of shittim wood, and its seat was worn with use. I sat there as the priests went on. From the far end of the hall, Mastanabal's voice broke the silence that seeped at last across the room. I could barely see him. The torchlight was not strong, and the smoke of cloying incense thick. Am I a superstitious man? I think not. But I bent down to adjust the twisted strap of one of my sandals. The mosaic on the floor was of pairs of opposing sacred fylfots. I saw my foot precisely in the middle of the unhallowed, unlucky one.

'Bostar of Chalcedon,' Mastanabal called out. 'We have turned to you for counsel in this hour. You have read the letter from the Roman Consul?'

'I have, Lord Sufet.'

'And your opinion is?'

'I know, or rather knew, Claudius Metellus Pulcher. He is equanimous, and true.'

'Not one of Cato's party?'

'No. He is his own man – although he thought the treaty after the last war was not fair to Rome. But before we turn to the Romans' three demands, may I ask, Elders of Carthage, something of you?'

I could see Mastanabal's shape lean forwards, and confer with those sitting next to him. He sat back in his chair. 'By all means.'

I stood up, and looked round me at the hundred Elders in the smoke and scented gloom. 'Is the Roman allegation true?' There was a buzz of voices round the room.

One of them to my left stood up. 'Stranger, I am Qart, Sufet of the harbour and our fleets – or, I should say, fleet, for as you know we have only trading ships, and none of war.' There was a murmur of assent round the room, and the stamping of feet. 'I swear by Moloch and by all the gods. We authorised no such attack.'

'But there are Carthaginian pirates to the east,' I replied, 'in Caria and Mysia, out of Rhodes and Crete.'

'That is true, but theirs is an ancient way of life, born not of Carthage but of Tyre. They glean their small pickings around Cyprus or off the coast of Cilicia, as they have always done,' Qart replied. 'In hundreds of years, they have never ventured west before. Why should they have done so now?'

'I see, I see,' I said. I sensed perfidy, but not here. 'Then you must reply in the strongest terms to Pulcher's second point. Insist that you know nothing of this at all. Suggest, in answer to your question, Qart—'

'Suggest what?' Mastanabal intervened.

'The truth. That these pirates may have been paid to attack, and by a Roman, to provoke war.'

'By Cato, you mean,' another Elder called.

'I would not go so far as to name him,' I said.

'Bostar of Chalcedon!' This was a new voice, deep and low. 'I am Abdoniba, and I lived in Rome for three years before the last war. The High Sufet speaks well of you. But surely the Romans will dismiss any such claim out of hand!'

'Cato's party will, yes,' I granted. 'But there are others.'

'Like who?' Abdoniba spat back.

'Like those who follow Lucius Valerius Flaccus, the Father of the Senate. He is one, I believe, trustworthy in that lair. So make your suggestion. If nothing else, that will divide the Romans. They will debate the question. You know how, if they have nothing else to discuss, they debate the existence of air.'

That brought some chuckles. I continued. 'And as they debate, we will win time to prepare.'

'Prepare, Bostar?' It was Mastanabal. 'Prepare? For what?'

'Prepare, Elders of Carthage,' I said, raising my voice, pushing from my plexus, 'for war.'

There was consternation in the room. Qart called out across the din. 'You are suggesting war?'

'No,' I replied. 'I want only peace. But I do not think we will have that unless the Romans know we are prepared for war.' I looked slowly round the Council chamber, and resumed my seat.

Discussion drifted back and forth across the room, until Mastanabal called matters to order. 'Next, Elders,' he declared, 'there is the question of the 10,000 gold *denarii*. Bostar, what's your view?'

'Simple. Pay it. Why, don't you have such a sum?'

'We do,' came a different voice from the corner to my right, an old one that quavered as it soared, 'but we don't. That is, the annual indemnity after the last war was fixed as a percentage of the reserves we declared.'

I understood. Why is little ever as it seems? A suckling child can trust the breast that feeds it, whilst it can. Is there nothing more? If Carthage paid the 10,000 gold *denarii*, a huge amount, it would be tantamount to admitting that the level of indemnity was based falsely, and should be raised. I sighed, and rubbed my eyes. 'Elders, how you extricate yourselves from this predicament is up to you. But pay you must, and straightaway. What about the wheat?'

'That is not an issue. We have had record harvests this year, and our silos are bursting. But the third demand?' Mastanabal asked. 'Who, Elders, will go as a hostage to the lions' den?'

I heard feet shuffle, saw heads shake. The silence was long, dismal and profound. Then from the shadows behind Mastanabal's chair, a man walked forward. He entered the circle of torchlight. 'Elders of Carthage,' the man said quietly, 'with your permission, I will go.' It was Astylax I saw.

Deposition preserved in the archives of Rome

Marcus Favonius Maximus, Aedile, to Gnaeus Flavius Sabinus, Praetor urbanus. This follows our conversation yesterday in the Forum, and constitutes an official complaint against my neighbour, Publius Cornelius Scipio, whose father Africanus I served. Because you say this is not a criminal matter, let this serve as intimation that on the next *dies faustus* I will be raising a civil action against Scipio. Since he moved into his father's villa, next to mine, my household and I have had barely a single night's sleep. His parties are wild and unseemly for someone of his station. People come that one would expect to meet in the Quirinal, but not here. Each night there is drinking, feasting and music, until well after dawn. Last night, for example, Scipio had a great bonfire in his garden. I smelled the smoke, of course, and roused my servants to fetch buckets of water and stand ready lest the fire should set light to my roof. But the noise grew so great I had a ladder brought and climbed up the wall between our properties. I saw masked men and women dancing round the bonfire as if in some Dionysiac orgy. This will not do. I cannot endure such a neighbour. Think of the influence on my children! Scipio must change his ways. Since my requests have not moved him, I will ensure that the law does.

From Hanno's memoir

For me those were halcyon times. I was enjoying my days at the school of the Spartan, Nicomachus. I loved the wrestling in particular, and became quite an adept of the javelin and spear. But what Bostar did not know is that, on my way home, I was seeing Fetopa, whose house was near.

An unusual question led me to understand all was not well, beyond my narrow mien. I had just returned. It was raining, and thunder cracked across the sky. I was wet. Bostar heard me close the door, I suppose, and came out from his room into the hall.

'Hanno,' he asked me, straight out, 'is there anything wrong with your penis?'

I blushed, confused. 'My penis? What do you mean?'

'Stop blushing, for heaven's sake!' Such curtness was not like him. I looked slowly at him, at his tight and furrowed brow. 'I am circumcised,' he went on. 'You are circumcised. Correct?'

'Correct, Bostar. But what do you mean?'

'I mean, Hanno, that we urinate straight into the hole. Is that not so?'

I should explain that Bostar was fastidious about these things. When we first took our house, it had the usual plain long drop. You squatted to defecate, or stood above it to urinate, often splashing the tiles. Bostar had a carpenter build a seat above it, with a lid. It would keep, he said, the flies away or down. It did.

'I'm sorry, Hanno,' he went on, his face relaxing. 'It has been a long day – and night. Xetha made our supper earlier. It's ready. Come and sit down, and I will tell you what I know.' Throwing my wet cloak into a corner, I followed him into the dining room and sat down on a couch. Its hessian scratched my dripping knees.

'Brr-h,' Bostar exclaimed. 'It's time we lit a fire. But let me explain. Someone, a man, has been here.'

'How do you know?'

'Urine. Round the base of the latrine. From a man with a foreskin, or an inflammation, which made him dribble. You and I, as it were, shoot straight. He didn't. I'm sorry, that's why I asked you.'

'But weren't you in all day?'

'No. I was out with Tancinus this afternoon.'

'When Xetha was off.'

'No. She wasn't here. At least she was, but she went home early. She has a heavy cold.' He sank his face into his hands, and rubbed his eyes with the heels of his hands. 'So, Hanno, there is the urine. And, though I can't be sure, I think someone has been at my desk, reading my journal, going through my papers.'

'What makes you think that?'

'A hunch, a sense, Hanno – a smell.'

'A smell?' I asked, bemused.

'Yes. When I came home, in my room I'm sure I smelled the faintest whiff of bergamot.' He sucked his teeth and rubbed his brow. Then Bostar brightened. 'But it's probably the lemon trees in our yard. Anyway, there's nothing wrong with me that won't be fixed by a good plate of Xetha's broth. The hearth should still be lit. Go and warm our soup, will you?'

Letter preserved in the archives of Neapolis

Labienus to Curtius. Thanks to your good offices and the help of Flaccus, it is done. Scipio took ship yesterday for Baetica. A tribe called the Darconi have rebelled for the fourth time in as many years. Under the proconsul Germanicus, our garrison at Corduba is to exterminate them, and Scipio is bound for there. He leaves late in the year. His crossing will be stormy, but frankly I think it will be good for him to be seasick for a few days. It will clear his blood of accumulated wine. I will shut up your house here, and return, with some relief I must confess, to mine in Capua where in time I hope to be able to greet Scipio, by then we trust a wiser and a better man, fulcrum of our hopes and of our dreams.

From Hanno's memoir

It was the cisterns that did it. That is where we walked and talked and played in private, Fetopa and I, when she was done with her diurnal duties in the High Sufet's palace and I had finished with my school. She knew a secret entrance, down a vennel by her house, and there we would sneak to raise the wooden hatch, climb down the mossed and ancient ladder, walk the miles of tunnels, play with the echoes of our voices, talk – and touch.

That first time was when the workmen almost caught us. Of course the cisterns and their connecting walkways had to be kept scrupulously clean. But dirt and rubbish fell in from the grilles in the streets above that let in light and air. It was this that these men were sent to take away. Fetopa heard them before I did.

'Quick, Hanno,' she said. 'There are people coming. Down here!' She pulled me after her, down a dark, damp passage to our left. It led nowhere. The cleaners, or they might have been inspecting engineers, were almost alongside. Fetopa pressed right back against the wall and tugged me to her, deep into the dark. That is when I felt her breasts, yielding and reforming against my back. The men passed. In my loins and in my belly, longing stirred. I turned, and pressed against her, my right hand reaching, lifting up her smock of cotton and tracing the curves of her buttocks, her hip, my fingers glancing on the undulations of her ribs until the thrilling, safe softness of her breast, my thumb on nipple, cupped home in my hand. She quivered, her head sinking onto my shoulder, and I hugged her to me with my left arm, to a sense of solace, to a sense completely sure.

The drip surprised me, condensation from the roof above us falling right onto my forehead. The spell was broken, but we both laughed as I wiped the water away. Fetopa shivered. 'Let's go, Hanno,' she said softly. 'It's damp in here.' We did go, but not before she reached up and kissed me, then I her, on nose and eyes and cheeks, my tongue running along her scar. We rejoined the world above us, and I ran home, rejoicing, sure that a covenant had been conceived.

Letter preserved in the military archives of Rome

Fistulus Aemelius Germanicus, proconsul in Baetica, to Claudius Metellus Pulcher, consul in Rome. Your Scipio has joined us. He drinks too much, and pines for Rome. But already the soldiers love him, and not just for his father's name. So do most of my officers, and not just for the imaginative games of dice he plays. Yesterday, we came upon a camp of the Darconi six days' march west of Corduba. You will be familiar with this type of fortification. They call them *crannochths*. Protected by a high wooden palisade, this was as strong a one as I have seen, a real vipers' nest, on an island a good eighty paces out in the middle of a fast flowing river, accessible only by a ford wide enough for one man at a time. But I could not leave it in our rear. The Darconi taunted us, and wounded three of my *hastati* with fusillades of stones – you will remember the deadly slings they use. I tried fire arrows but, the Darconi having no shortage of water, to no discernible avail. Then I lost six men, one to spear (he got the closest) and five to arrows on the ford. It proved impossible, being so narrow, for a *testudo* to be formed.

Resigning myself to the inevitable, I gave the order for circumvallation on both sides of the river, called, for the information of your cartographers, the Gabro. My quartermaster assured me we had enough munitions for a three-week siege, assuming we availed ourselves of the plentiful local hares – not a prospect, for you know my distaste for the rank meat of that rodent, that I enjoyed. Still, I comforted myself with the thought that these barbarians rarely prepare themselves beyond the needs of a few days. Assuming they were not cannibals, having satisfied myself of the advice of one of my centurions, a freshriver fisherman himself before he served, that the river flowed too fast to afford the Darconi any chance of catching fish with which to feed themselves, having checked our pickets were alert to attack from our rear and having tested myself our system of signals from these pickets to my centurion, I retired to my tent and, having eaten the regulation millet bread and dried pork with, for my first time some relish after many years in the field, given my aforesaid aversion to the prospect of jugged hare [*I cannot resist this one interspersion. This is Latin for you, dense and constipated and always tripping on its own toes. I thank Hera I am bound for Corinth – or at least for that of it which is still there – and Greek, a language which inhales.*], I unrolled my copy of Ennius' *Annales*. Do you know it? He actually tutored Scipio, I am told, and is said to be composing a panygeric on Africanus. I am of course too polite to enquire. Anyway, I recommend his hexameters as every bit as good as Homer's, I should say.

But no sooner had I settled to my Ennius than the flap of my tent opened. Scipio appeared. 'Forgive me, sir, but it's the mosquitoes.'

'The mosquitoes, tribune? Have you been drinking – again?' I replied.

'Unfortunately not, sir. But you must have noticed.'

As it happens, I had. My inspection of the pickets at sundown had been, I can confess to you in confidence as my late uncle's friend, perfunctory. Great clouds of the damn brutes followed me like fog and clogged my nostrils and my ears. The legionaries lacked, we being under marching orders and short of gear and summer being the time of year, the luxury of a tent to exclude mosquitoes and were bedded under stars.

'They are intolerable, sir,' Scipio went on. 'We need to move to higher ground, away from water.'

'Brilliant, tribune,' I replied acidly. 'And leave the Darconi here?'

'Certainly not, sir. I have a plan.'

I put my Ennius aside. 'Come in, tribune,' I said, 'and sit down.'

His proposal was audacious, but straightforward. He had clearly thought it through, and wanted only twenty men, of his choosing, to effect it. He wanted to attack the camp of the enemy, there and then, in the dark.

'I will cross first, sir, taking a rope. I will secure that on the other side, and the men will use it to guide their way across.'

'And if you slip off the ford?' I asked him.

'Then, sir, my plan will have failed.'

'And if the Darconi see you?'

'I don't know,' he replied, 'but I should think the same applies. I wouldn't have suggested this were it not a moonless night.'

I sat back and crossed my arms. Could I afford to lose him? These things happen in war. Could I afford to lose another twenty men? With the mosquitoes as many as they were, there was every probability of fever killing even more.

'Very well, tribune,' I said. 'Proceed.'

From the shelter of some scrub, squatting with his team of men, their armour off, their arms muffled, I saw Scipio leave, the rope around his waist. After a tense wait, the rope tugged. One of the soldiers tied our end to a tree and off they went, one by one, the last carrying no arms but a light ladder strapped to his back.

Scipio scaled the palisade with that, he reported later, cut the throat of one sleeping guard, opened the gate and let his men in. I had heard nothing, what with the river running and the mosquitoes buzzing in my ears. But then I smelled the smoke and saw the fires.

Covered in blood, Scipio first, all the men returned. As they came splashing, cheering to the bank, Scipio reported calmly: 'Mission complete, sir. No casualties on our side, but thirty-one Darconi dead.'

'You took no prisoners?'

'No, sir.' He stood at attention before me in the dark, his face illuminated by the burning camp. 'At least, no men, sir. But we did bring this.'

He gestured, and I saw the young woman, bedraggled, sobbing, sullen, her hands tied, the nipples of her pert breasts stiff under her wet shift. 'She has a little Latin, Sir. Her name is Sophonisa, and she says she is a princess of these people. I thought she would make a useful hostage—'

'You thought, tribune, you thought!' I replied. 'I don't want to treat with the Darconi. I want to wipe them out! Now we're going to be encumbered by a bloody girl!'

'Begging your pardon, sir, but she is a woman. And I will assume full responsibility for her, proconsul. And, sir?'

'Yes? What is it?'

'May I assume that, in the morning, we move camp to higher ground?'

Such, Pulcher, is the Scipio you have sent me. Anyway, as you will I am sure think right, I have awarded him the *corona vallaris*, the crown for conspicuous courage in scaling a camp wall under assault – which he didn't, but he would have done. Kindly inform the Senate that more honours have fallen to an illustrious line.

From Hanno's memoir

They came for me at dawn, two servants of the Sufet, mute and deaf but, as I was to find out, fit. I had not eaten, as I had been told. The litter left us at the inner western gate. We walked from there, through the next gate, across the walkway that bridged the moat then through the final wall. As we moved along the causeway and the road that began at the end of the lagoon, I regretted the thick, clumsy boots I had been told to wear. When we veered off it into the low hills of scree, I began to understand. The sun grew hot. Ahead of me, the servants did not check. Acarpous shrubs and short, spiny trees chafed at our legs. I would have welcomed a breeze.

We were almost round the side of Carthage, having swung west and south to avoid the marshes into which a man could sink and not be seen again. Across the bay before us rose the foothills and the peaks of Jebel-bou-Kournine.

We stopped at midday to drink sweet water from a spring. Apart from that grove of lime and pine, the land was flat and bare, the beach now to the north of us long and clean. My sweat dried, but not for long. Soon, we began to climb. Although the path was clear, the trees above and around it meant we often had to stoop and even crawl. Monkeys chattered. Ibics hooted. Mosasaurus lizards lay languid then darted, green and red and grey. I saw one black viper scuttling away. Plants of vervain studded the sward, and sycamine clustered on any open ground.

Puffing, panting, legs aching, I followed on the servants, moving like gazelles. Mid-afternoon. A clearing. A rivulet and very welcome water. Far behind, below us, through the trees, across the blue and silver sea I saw Carthage, and the pall of cooking fires hanging over her on a still windless day. We climbed on, the mountain now so steep I was on hands and legs, boots slipping, stones sliding down the precipitate way. The mountain narrowed. We went up and up a vertiginous ridge, the twin, curling peaks above it clear before me, even through my sweaty, dusty eyes.

At the top, just as the sun was fading, the servants left me to go down. I sat where they pointed and waited, my stomach grumbling, looking round. I could see far over the dot of Carthage, way beyond her to Cap Bon and beyond that, or was it just a shadow, the mass of Sicily looming in the darkening sea. But my eyes kept returning to the narrow path before me, snaking round the first of the peaks to a paved circle, on which stood a low hut of stones and beyond that to the unlit beacon before the second peak, and after that a sheer drop to below.

The sun set. I must have slept. I woke up, shivering, trembling to the beacon blazing above me and belching acrid smoke that stung my throat and lungs. Then I heard the drum, deep and pulsing, around, before, behind me, smoke and nausea and sound. It stopped. I looked forwards to the circle, squinting in the fickle firelight to be sure. An old, grimalkin of a crone, stooped and haggard, hair dishevelled, shoeless, stood there, waving at me to come on.

I stood up, felt my legs weak and sore beneath me. Swaying, uncertain, I edged my way along the narrow path, knowing the death on either side, until I stood before her and she raised her head and cackled to the sudden wind. Sparks and smuts flew all around us as her laugh grew shriller still. It stopped as suddenly as if a demon had stolen it. Lisping, lilting, eyes rolling, 'You are Hanno Barca?' she wailed.

'I am.'

'Take off your shirt.'

I did, and threw it, saw it wafting on the winds. Then, I only glimpsed it coming, she hit me with a headed stick. I felt the tearing cross my chest, the ripping of a lion's claws, knew the pain exploding in my brain.

The rest I cannot remember. Only fragments, flashes. Swinging, flailing, crying, imploring, pleading, refusing, fighting, begging death to take me in. Lightning streaking, figments falling, Capua, my father who would never come.

The sun, sun, burning, burning, forcing me to open up my eyes. The flies, flies, buzzing, buzzing at the blood dried and drying down my chest, smearing my thighs. That is what I woke to, what my conscious memory tells me of the Passage of Ordeal. I was slumped at the base of the still blazing beacon. Through each of my breasts there ran a wooden spike, and a rope led up from both ends of these. I strained to follow the four ropes' lines, threading into one that ran up to a bracket and the sort of pulley builders use. I was suspended there, I thought, swinging between the sacred peaks. Then, fleeing the pain, I returned to the shadows of Eschmoun.

I saw visions. People visited me, ghosts and spectres from beyond the River of Forgetfulness, Ashroket in our Punic tongue. I was with my grandfather, Hamilcar, as he died in Spain, his last words to my father 'Rome! Rome!' I was with my father as he cut his throat, naked and alone in a room in Bithynia, rather than submit to Rome. I saw the sadness, the suffering in his eyes. I reached out to him to staunch the blood – but he was gone and I was with him and my mother as they made me. I felt my father's loneliness, my mother's taking it to her. I saw her crying as my father moved up and down in her, but I knew her tears were tears of joy, not pain.

Like a wind, like a shooting star I travelled far and long. I saw battles at sea, on land. I saw crucifixions, disembowellings. I heard the tramp, tramp of armies marching to war, the trumpeting of elephants. I smelled the smells of sweat and defecating fear.

I suppose they cut me free, the same servants, returned, and carried me back down. I remember only small parts of the journey back to Carthage, as one glimpses stars in the sky on a night of storm. But the certainty has never left me. I knew what had to be done.

From Bostar's journal

In the streets, the market, the people talk of nothing else. After centuries of subservience and tribute, a desert tribe they call the Eraxth have rebelled, burning the farms and houses round Hadrumetum. A farmer who survived has brought the news. Can we see in this, I wonder, the hand of Rome? For my part, I am concerned about the forests. It is from those around Hadrumetum that the wood comes for the galleys we are having built. The rebellion must be repressed. The city guard is small, but well trained and armed. I will ask Mastanabal what he plans.

Report filed in the archives of the Senate of Rome

Pius Lucerius Sura, Governor of Syracuse, to Lucius Valerius Flaccus in Rome. I write this report in order that there should be no misunderstanding. Your legate has criticised my actions as heavy handed. With respect, he was not here.

The riot was not, as he has called it, a 'minor matter' to which I 'over-reacted'. It was bad enough before I stopped it. I believe your legate has supplied you with a list of the dead, of the homes and property destroyed. As far as my enquiries can establish, it began as a scuffle in the market. A Roman accused a Carthaginian butcher of selling him short measure. Tempers flared. By the time the guard were called, it had become a running brawl, with carts and stalls being overturned, some even fired, the Carthaginians and Romans guilty in equal parts.

I cannot establish when arms first were drawn, but I did establish by whom: a Carthaginian knife maker, called Agoun, was attested by several witnesses as distributing axes and swords. My guard had a hard time of it, restoring order. Indeed, three of them were killed. It was only when I ordered in the cavalry that the crisis passed.

I had Agoun crucified, and two of his men. As for Romans, I could find no particular miscreant, so have punished no one in particular. I have the whole city under curfew.

You will have read my recommendations, beginning over two years ago, that we repatriate all the Carthaginians, not only from Syracuse but from the whole of Sicily. I know the views of the Senate: that we need their money and their skills. But this is proof that the two peoples cannot live as one. There is too much festering ill-feeling, after centuries of war.

From Bostar's journal

He was acclaimed today. I have seen many ceremonies in my time. This was fine, in the city's huge, central square. On the steps that lead up to the Senate, before the people and most of the Elders, to the sound of cymbals, kinnors and citharas, Mastanabal proclaimed Hanno to be Hanno Barca, son of Hannibal, son of Hamilcar.

So another part of my plan takes its proper place. But I felt no satisfaction. Hanno has been cold and often sullen since he endured the Passage of Ordeal. I asked him about it. All he said to me, coldly, was: 'You are not a Carthaginian, Bostar. You wouldn't understand.'

As I watched the ceremony, my mind was elsewhere. Early this morning before the naming, Hanno sleeping, I was working on plans to deepen the western moat, collating Tancinus' and my ideas. There was a sharp knock at the door. I opened it. 'Sphylax!' I said. 'What brings you here?'

He was looking worried, strained. 'Come in,' I said, stepping back.

'I will, Bostar, but only for a moment.'

I closed the door. 'Tea?' I offered. 'I have a kettle on the hearth.'

He shook his head. 'No, Bostar, thank you. Let me get straight to the point, before I go to the *mehashebim*. Do you remember the plans I showed you of the city's cisterns?'

'Yes. Of course I do. A whole network under the city. Magnificent. But why do you ask?'

'Because they're gone. I went to my office early this morning to consult them. We had a leak reported, late last night.

All the cellars of the eastern houses are flooded, so it must be serious.'

'And?'

'And, Bostar, I couldn't find the plans. I looked everywhere. They're gone.'

'Extraordinary,' I said, sitting down on the hall chair. 'Tell me, Sphylax, who saw them last, or who has seen them since you showed them to me?'

'I have, of course.'

'But apart from you?'

'Astylax. He came to consult them yesterday morning. Said the Sufet wanted a few things checked.'

'And you stayed with him?'

'No, as it happens. I had a meeting to go to. I left him alone. Bostar, what's wrong?'

'What is wrong, Sphylax, is that yesterday evening Astylax left Carthage.'

'Left? Where has he gone?'

I stood up, feeling old and cold and weary. I rubbed my face, and raised my head to him. 'Astylax has gone, Sphylax, to Rome.'

From Hanno's memoir

It was to Nicomachus I owe the ruse. But it was Halax who chose the ground. With six hundred of the city Guard, all mounted, and twenty elephants we had pursued the Eraxth for eleven days as they zig-zagged south and west. The rolling scrubland gave way to desert sands and burning sun. Our lips cracked. Our hands blistered on the reins. Halax grew concerned about water for us, and fodder for our elephants and horses. 'If we can't catch them,' Nicomachus said, 'we'll have to let them catch us.' He explained his plan. Halax nodded. 'I know just the place,' he said.

I sent two scouts ahead to ensure the Eraxth were not near, or cutting back. I had a hundred of our men camp in a hollow, ringed by dunes, their orders to make as many fires as they could and as large a camp. To three of them I gave a clay whistle, made by Halax's mother. We had tested them in Carthage. Their pure, high note sounded far and could, as we had proved in an experiment, be heard even above the noise of Carthage's market.

The rest of us retired to a ravine. There was scrub there, and Halax had the elephants lie down. So did we, and waited, bar two pickets I posted to let us know if the Eraxth had found us, or been taken in. I was relying on the hope that, if they came back for us when they discovered we were no longer following them, they would come from the south where they had last been seen. The ravine where we were hiding was to the north of the hollow and the dunes.

Dusk came and went. The stars grew bright, the night cold.

I chewed on dry meat, sipped a little water and remembered my dreams from Eschmoun. Around me came men's snores, the whinnying of horses and the low grumble of elephants. I stayed awake by counting stars.

Letter preserved in the archives of Rome

Cato to Spurius Lingustus. You did well. I have another small commission for you, on even more generous terms. Go to Sicily, and start in Syracuse. There has been trouble there, as you may have heard. When the moment seems appropriate, fire a Roman ship, a merchantman ideally, in the harbour there and leave at once. Then do the same, one week later, in whichever of the island's other harbours as seems best; a week after that, do the same a third and final time.

By the time you read this, I will be gone, first to inspect my new farm for fish, and then to my home in the country where, if necessary, your messengers can find me. I have not seen my wife and son for far too long. Anyway, having started a fire, I will leave it now to burn.

From Hanno's memoir

Perhaps I dozed. The stars had set, and my cloak was wet with dew when I started to the whistles' shrill. Everyone was on their feet and running for the horses. I passed Halax urging the elephants up and on. We scrambled up the bank, across the ground and up the dunes. The fires gave light enough to see our men in a phalanx, as Nicomachus had taught them, bristling like a porcupine with spears as Eraxth beset them, too close for bows but wielding their crescent swords.

I gave no command. As one man, we dismounted, throwing our cloaks to the ground. Down we charged, our war cry 'Carth-age!' ringing in our ears. It is a madness, battle. Once you are committed, there can be no plan but only the will of man against man. The Eraxth turned. We are outnumbered, I remember thinking, but then I was thrusting, parrying and a scimitar swept past my left ear. I dropped down and rose using my knees and took that man, as Nicomachus had advised us, with a straight thrust just under his cuirass into his groin. I exulted in that penetration, the only thing as sweet as sex that I have ever known.

In the end, they were surrounded. The perhaps three hundred Eraxth surviving just threw down their swords and dropped their wicker shields. Some fell on their knees, muttering imprecations. We backed away, and Halax led the elephants down. The Eraxth who tried to run we speared or shot with bows. Most, though, lay down to accept their fate. Halax had said their will to fight or live could end as quickly as a summer storm. He was right. But that did not prevent their screams as the elephants, trumpeting and rising on their hind legs, trampled and pulped them. As the sun rose over the bowl, the sand shone red with blood.

From Bostar's journal

Astylax's treachery perturbs and preoccupies me – although Mastanabal insists we cannot be sure. I am, and he will find out, in time. But what concerns me more is that I was so wrong about the man. Has my judgement failed me? Is my whole design too flawed? Because he must be elected to the Senate and propose and carry a new treaty of perpetual peace between equals, much hinges now on Scipio. I wrote six days ago to Labienus. My courier was due to return yesterday. He must have been delayed; I hope only by storm.

At least the construction of the war galleys is going well. Ten are ready, and it will be over twenty before the moon turns again. I must talk to Mastanabal about sailors and rowers. Otherwise I am much engaged with Tancinus, who continues to impress me, and with buying Hanno his own house. He thinks I have not noticed. But unless I am much mistaken (again), he will soon be taking himself a wife.

From Hanno's memoir

It was my first formal meeting with the High Sufet since my proc-
lamation, and since we had returned from punishing the Eraxth.
'But they cannot just crucify people, Mastanabal!' I insisted. He
had told me the news from Syracuse.

'They can and they do,' he replied. 'That is the law of Rome.'

'And so?'

'And so, until I can arrange a meeting with Rome's Senate or
its legates, we must protect our citizens meanwhile, wherever
they are. That means removing from Sicily as many of our
people as want to come back to Carthage. My sister and her
husband, for example, are there. So, even this late in the year
I have arranged for a fleet of five transports to go to Syracuse,
Hanno, and—'

He leaned forward to stoke the brazier, then sat back in his
chair.

'And?'

'Hanno, who will lead them?'

'I will, Sufet. I know now who I am.'

He stared at me. He mused.

'Very well. Talk to the Romans, especially the governor, Lucerius
Sura. He is said to be a fair and honest man. Find out what is going
on. You leave tomorrow morning. That is all.'

The Sufet nodded my dismissal. I got up to go, and was almost
at the door.

'Oh, and Hanno?' Mastanabal called.

'Yes, Lord Sufet?'

'Be careful.'

'I will be. Rest assured.'

I was careful, but no man can avoid what some call coincidence, and I the will of the gods.

I in the third ship, we were just entering the mouth of Syracuse's harbour when we saw fire run up the rigging of a galley, clearly Roman by its fit and flags. We were closing on it, moored at the first wharf, and I could see the fire brigades and soldiers running along the quay, the blaze catching hold when, from the walls above us, the catapults began to fire. The first volley missed us. The second did not. The transport in front of us took a direct hit in the side. Struck by an oval black stone, our own foremast came crashing down, knocking our drummer overboard. 'Helmsman, about! Oars, belay!' our captain shouted beside me.

'You can't!' I cried to him. A huge stone thudded into the water beside us, drenching us with spray.

'Forgive me, sir, but do you have a better idea?' the captain replied, and he was gone to take the helm.

I looked back one last time as we turned the point for home. Through the smoke of the burning vessel, I saw our two galleys being pounded with stones. On a turn of the breeze, I heard our sailors' screams. That is how I came back to Carthage the same day I had gone. Four ships had left, but only two returned. That, I knew, was the least of our loss.

Letter found among Cato's papers

My dearest wife. I may never send this to you, but I write it to still my racing mind. It has been frantic here, with senators coming and going all day, and yesterday too, shut in with Cato, discussing things in hushed but earnest tones. Cato has just left. He will be gone for at least a month, he said, to see to his affairs. But just as he was about to leave, a courier came. He read the despatch. Its contents interested him greatly, and having finished he sat deep in reflection for a while. Then, he rose to go. The despatch was on his desk. His last act was to throw it on the brazier, which was low.

Perhaps I should not have saved it from the flames. But I did, and I read it, before I put it back to burn. It was from Mastanabal, High Sufet of Carthage, to Cato, Flaccus and the Senate of Rome. It insisted that the burning of a Roman galley in the harbour of Syracuse was not the work of Carthaginian hands. It asked for a legation to be allowed to come to Rome from Carthage, and assure the Senate and People that Carthage wants peace, not war.

Cato should at least have let his colleagues see this. If I speak out, I will be ruined, and you too. But is that the price I have to pay for justice? What am I to do?

From Bostar's journal

Tancinus' argument and figures are irrefutable. The city guard is only a thousand men, not enough to man one wall. Carthage has always relied on mercenaries. Yet the treaty insists that Carthage cannot have an army, without the prior consent of Rome. That of course would be denied. I have spoken to Nicomachus, in the strictest confidence. He assures me that he could raise an army of ten thousand in three weeks, and twenty thousand in five. The slingers would be Balearics, the infantry Greek, the cavalry Numidian and so on. I must marshal my arguments carefully, before I put them to Mastanabal.

Letter found among Cato's papers

Sempronia, wife of Cato Censorius, to Speusippus in Rome. My husband is unwell. He has a high fever, and cannot return to Rome and his duties. Inform the relevant authorities. I will write again when he is better. That may be some time.

Letter preserved in the archives of Neapolis

Flaccus to Curtius. The last time I asked you to come to Rome it was as a favour. Now it is a command. The Republic needs your experience and counsel. Come quickly, my old friend. I will tell you why when I see you, but I fear we are on the brink of war. Meanwhile, you should know that young Scipio has returned from his latest campaign, this time in Gaul. Once again, he has covered himself in glory. The Senate, despite the opposition of Cato's party, proposes to promote him to the rank of praetor. I concur.

Letter preserved in the archives of Neapolis

Flaccus to Curtius. Ignore my last letter. You are too late. Stay where you are. If anything, I will come to Neapolis when the final stages of this play – I know not whether it is tragedy or comedy – are past. Another of our ships was burned in Sicily. The Senate's mood darkened, and then we heard of a third, and then an even more serious matter. The wife of Sura, Governor of Syracuse, was in their villa in the hills. The servants who survived are clear. It was by Carthaginians she was raped and killed. What is going on?

Anyway, it was Pulcher who moved the formal motion for war. This was no bellicosity from Cato. He was not here, and has not been for weeks. He is on his farm, unwell. The vote? There were thirty-two abstentions, but *nem.con.dic.* So is the die cast. Tomorrow in the Forum the Pontifex will proclaim *casus belli*, and then open the gates of Mars.

[I omit several pages about mobilisation. Like most Romans, Flaccus and Curtius are soldiers at heart, and Flaccus waxed lyrical about legions and levies; about which auxiliaries should accompany whom. Rome's mobilisation of course took months, but was as always almost astonishingly thorough. I have even found papers about how many pounds of nails each legion was assigned. I have read the records of the Senate's long debates about boots, and the relative merits of millet and barley bread. Again, it might seem that the final campaign against Carthage was brought about by Cato. But it was the work of more minds than his. In war one man may light the taper. But it is the will of many that it burns.]

All that remains is for the Senate to choose the commander. We reconvene for that tomorrow at noon. Pulcher must be the favourite, but Germanicus is said to want the job as well. I hope not to have to vote, but if I do I will cast for Pulcher. I will write again tomorrow when I know. Consider yourself fortunate not to be here.

Letter preserved in the citadel of Carthage

Labienus in Capua to Bostar, in great haste. My friend. I have the gravest news from Curtius, who is in Neapolis. The Romans are mobilising. Tomorrow a fleet is to begin assembling at Ostia, enough to carry eight legions to Carthage. I would be crucified were this message to reach the wrong hands, so I am sending it with Artixes. He is to stay with you. You will need his services, if there is to be a siege. Apurnia asks me to ask you to tell Hanno she loves him, and always will.

Letter preserved in the archives of Rome

Sempronia to Lucius Valerius Flaccus, Father of the Senate of Rome. My husband Cato died last night. In my grief, I want to say little more. Your officials will, I presume, attend to all the formalities. But please note that I want my husband buried here. As for his last words, I wish it were otherwise, but here they are. He was raving, delirious with fever. He sat up suddenly, called out *'Delanda est Carthago!'*, collapsed back, coughed, looked up at me, and was no more.

Letter preserved in the archives of Neapolis

Flaccus to Curtius. Now I have seen it all. I was hoping to keep proceedings short. They were, but no thanks to me. I had just begun the ritual stuff about choosing commanders in times of war when Antoninus stood up. 'Father of the House,' he said, 'before you go any further I have a motion here, already signed by a binding majority of members, and so—'

'And sponsored by?' I interrupted, annoyed.

'By Marcus Porcius Cato, Father, *in absentia.*'

'Oh, yes. And what does this motion move, Antoninus?'

He flourished the scroll before him. 'It appoints a commander of our army which is to destroy Carthage, and root out the evil which has continued since the last war.'

'And that man is?'

'Publius Cornelius Scipio, Father, Africanus minor.'

The House broke into uproar. I didn't check the propriety of the document. I couldn't care.

The first ship our fleet intercepted was a quinquereme, out of Carthage by its course, new and fast, but not fast enough to outrun a wind that favoured Rome. On board was a Spartan, Nicomachus. He refused to talk. Scipio simply asked him which limb he would prefer to lose first. On Scipio's word that he could go free, he told us. He was on his way to raise a mercenary army for Carthage. So are matters of the utmost moment decided not by people or potentates, but by the wind. As for the Spartan, Scipio had him thrown overboard. 'I know Spartans can fight,' he said. 'But can they swim?'

The troops took heart, I heard, as the word spread from ship to ship. Thanks to Astylax, we knew how few there would be to defend Carthage's walls. Now we knew no mercenary army would take us in the rear. By nightfall, our fleet was moored within the bay of Carthage.

Letter preserved in the citadel of Carthage

Publius Cornelius Scipio Africanus to Hanno Barca. Thanks to Labienus, I feel I know you. I feel sometimes I am you. Thanks to Labienus, I feel I know Bostar, who may have meant otherwise but has brought me here. Sometimes I curse him. Thanks to Astylax, I know of your wife and children, of Mastanabal and your Council, of Massinissa. Thanks to the reports my father lodged and to Astylax, though I despise him, I have detailed plans of Carthage. I know of your walls and cisterns, your secret stores. I know how many men you have. I know your position. You know Rome. Until the stars are overturned in the heavens, she will be here.

Rome wants to destroy you. I know that I do not. Our fathers fought. Both lost, in their different ways. That is enough. Intercede with Mastanabal and the Elders of the Council. I beg you to surrender. Just open your gates, or the harbour, and not a hair of any of you will be harmed. I will force our Senate to grant you generous terms. By our fathers' shades, I swear.

From Bostar's journal

We are all exhausted. No one in this city has done more than snatch at sleep for many days. Tancinus is a marvel. He trains five hundred citizens a day. Hanno is in charge of armaments. To make balls for the catapults, we are even melting down the city's silver and gold. Fetopa organises the women. We have many bows, but no strings. To make them the women of Carthage have all cut off their hair – bar Fetopa. I saw the women beg her not to, so that they might have hope for when theirs grows again. Halax is in charge of all the city's animals. His elephants work wonders, moving munitions everywhere. Artixes has taken command of our hospitals, nurses and doctors. My responsibility is stores and food. The other Elders fill the temples with their dreams and pious prayers. And Mastanabal? He spends much of his time in the city's cemetery. Staring at what will be his own sarcophagus, he broods.

Letter found among Cato's papers

Cato the Censor to Massinissa, King of the Libycians. My legate tells me that you have agreed. If we ever attack Carthage, you will not come to her defence, neither by sea nor land. With this letter comes your gold. Sign this letter on the bottom, as proof that you accept these terms, and return it to me.

Letter delivered to Scipio at camp on the landward plain of Carthage, and now lodged with papers here

Hanno Barca to Scipio. I do not know you, and it is fruitless to wish I did. Without my knowing it, you came to be at the bottom of my mind, perhaps not least because you are a bastard, as am I. But we have gone astray, and showers of time and place have poured between us. You will never rise to the surface, although my hands should be hauling ceaselessly. I am only what other people have told you my father was. I pity you. Fate and the gods have made us what we are. They will determine what will be.

When my messenger returns, our western gates will open, and close again, for the last time. Treat with Mastanabal if you want to try. My way is set. My mind is clear. Perhaps you are different, only half Roman. I do not know. But rather than submit to Rome, my father Hannibal took his own life. If I have to, so will I. The cycle turns. Let it be.

Horror does not sharpen the senses. It blunts them. I saw things to burn the brain, and yet my memory is bovine. Let me see if I can make it stir. For the siege of Carthage, Scipio had a clear, agreed, considered plan to which the Carthaginian deserter Astylax contributed a great deal. But in such matters, the Romans are a machine. They have manuals of siege warfare, you know, ponderous things, in the Roman way taking the best of what others have learned and making it their own.

Indeed the bibliography of besiegement is already long. One of my countrymen, Aineias Tacitus, an Arcadian from Stymphalos, wrote an excellent and now standard work one hundred and fifty years ago. Scipio has a copy here. It is called Poliorcetica, *or 'How to survive under siege'. As that of Carthage unfolded, I often wondered if its leaders were sitting, as our soldiers laboured, reading Aineias.*

Fire was out, we agreed on the voyage. The city would be very hard to burn. So was mining. Astylax assured Scipio that the western moat had been so deepened as to make tunnels impossible. What the Romans often do, when their own lines of supply, as in this case, are clear is shut the besieged city or town or camp off, and let disease, hunger or thirst, usually all three, do their work for them. Again, this did not apply. According to Astylax, Carthage could survive on its resources for years.

But what about disease, I asked. We could catapult dead cows over their walls, I said. Astylax argued that would be pointless, the city being underpopulated without an army and having much space to burn or bury all the dead cows we could throw at them.

Then what about bribery, I asked. I pointed out that the great Alexander said the best way to take cities is with gold. Astylax was not amused. We had with us, it seemed, Carthage's only traitor – although I found it hard to believe that everyone in Carthage agrees with Plato: the way to become rich is not to increase your possessions, but to decrease your desires. Still, I kept my thoughts to myself.

We had also rejected escalade. Long before we got to Carthage, our engineers had calculated that the ladders and sambucas necessary to mount a wall ninety feet high would be far too long. They would be unable to take the weight of two men, let alone whole maniples.

Towers too were considered, and dismissed. The only possible way to take Carthage was from the south-west. That, of course, meant the lagoon. That meant the ground would be too soft to support the weight of the huge tower that would have been necessary. I was disappointed, I confess. I had imagined a huge helepolis, like that made by Demetrius the Besieger. We could have drained the lagoon, but Scipio was advised that would take too long.

So there we were, sixty thousand soldiers, five thousand pioneers, I never did establish just how many sailors, and all the apparatus and arsenal – rams, onagers, catapults, grapplers, mantlets, sheds and shields – that the might of Rome could command.

But Rome besieged Carthage, in the end, with a lesser, ancient implement – the spade. Our deliberations on the spot merely confirmed the Senate's prior plans. Scipio decided, and I believe he was right, that the only way to take Carthage was by a ramp. So, for four weary months, in shifts of night and day the Roman army dug.

It was a desperate business, though. First the Romans had to breach the outer wall. Because of the many shields, protective mantlets and sheds required, progress was very slow. We lost many men. However good your shields and screens, the legs holding or moving them have to be exposed. The Carthaginian catapulters became adept at shooting their stones low and short, so that they bounced and skipped into our ranks, smashing many shins. The soldiers lived then, but most died later of gangrene.

Bridging the moat, behind sheds of timber crossed with iron and protected from fire by thick leather hides, was going well – until concerted catapult balls brought the main shed tumbling down. A new and stronger one proved adequate, and the bridge was finished in a day. The rams had harder work with the inner wall. It was stronger, and the Carthaginians rained down incessant fire.

To draw defenders away, Scipio ordered a simultaneous naval attack on the seaward wall with ship-borne onagers and rams. By the time the Carthaginians realised it was a ruse, we had broken through. But the land beyond the second wall rose steeply to the last. The Carthaginians had peppered it with sharpened stakes, covered with iron hooks and caulked with razor shell. It proved impossible, there being no room between the stakes and under constant fire, to construct a screen. By the evening of each day, there would be twenty, thirty legionaries impaled. Only under cover of darkness could their bodies, dead or dying, be removed. The ground grew slippery with blood, and clouds of flies brought new misery to the men. It took our legions nine whole days to clear that way.

The engineers constructed the largest shed the world can ever have seen. It took three thousand men to push it, inch by cursing inch, into place. Then the digging began, the soil and rock then having to be carried with great labour and difficulty in baskets along the causeway. Scipio's foraging parties scoured the country-side for donkeys and mules. In the blood and sweat of many men, the ramp began to rise.

The Carthaginians grew ever more ingenious. When there was wind, they poured down basket after basket of burning sand. The eddies carried enough of it behind and under the screen. Men ran screaming from the work, tearing off their clothes and, from the walls, arrows poisoned with arsenic brought them down. They died dreadful deaths, choking on their own tongues and retching blood as their faces turned green. Whole cohorts were on burial duty. Two protested. Scipio had them decimated, each tenth man left swinging on the gallows on the causeway until the crows and carrion had stripped them clean.

Each time we began to raise the screen the defenders boiled great vats of viscous fenugreek and dropped them down, making the heaving men lose their footholds. They used ropes of burning tar which snaked and insinuated their way behind the screen, or through the grilles it had to have for light. They threw down huge amphorae of water, turning our position into a muddy swamp. One day the shed slipped, crushing two hundred and eleven men. Far beyond our camp, in a bowl of silent, sullen hills, Scipio had yet more pits dug for the Roman dead. But still the rampart rose.

One day, our scouts led into camp a large caravan, captured on its way back from Senegalia. There were over two hundred camels, each carrying sacks of topaz. Scipio ordered an assembly. From the rostrum, he promised each cohort a pound of the jewels for every foot the rampart rose. That brought a cheer. What matters to most men is money, now as of yore.

From Bostar's journal

My only surprise is that he had not ordered earlier what I had long dreaded. The *tophet*, or ritual infanticide, is what Carthaginians have always done in times of crisis. They believe it propitiates their gods. Children are cast into the great bronze arms of a statue of Moloch, through which they slip into a burning pit below. I was with Mastanabal on the inner western wall, looking out at the vast Roman camp beyond the lagoon, when he told me a *tophet* was to be held. I protested about killing innocent children. I said Carthage might need them if we survived the siege.

'But we won't use healthy children,' the High Sufet replied.

'Then?' I asked, puzzled.

'When I told you about our treatment of deformed children, Bostar, it was not entirely true. We keep some of them for just such an occasion. Do you want to see?'

I followed him and two stewards down, down into long passages and chambers under the city until I was struck by a sudden smell of sweat and excrement. One of the stewards passed nosegays around, and unlocked a large, studded door. Now I have seen hell. In a large room, lit only by one grille, its floor covered with stinking straw, I saw over a hundred children, hunchbacked, mutant, crippled, maimed, packed together like fowls, cheeping like chicks, creeping back away from us in fear.

I wanted to be sick. I wanted air. I turned, and ran back the way we had come. What is it that I have tried to preserve? Have I been a fool? Have I been naïve?

Curious to a Greek, because we are uneasy with abstractions, the Romans have a concept called 'clementia'. When the siege began, it was in the air. Scipio even sent to Rome for more transports in order to be able to ship away the Carthaginian survivors of the siege: to be sold as slaves, no doubt, but to be alive. He talked to his commanders about preventing rape, pillage and so on.

I am not sure when the mood turned. The change came from the dreadful privations and labour of the besiegers, almost imperceptibly, as a winter dawn. There were some desertions. Scipio had the men pursued, caught, and crucified. The whole army grew silent, sour. Men worked and ate and slept and worked and died.

So when the rampart was finally finished and the assault took place, I expected some breaches of discipline. But when I entered Carthage, on horseback, through the open western gate, in the early evening, six hours after Rome's army had taken the city by storm, nothing had prepared me for what I saw.

The carnage was general. But at such times the human mind fixes on the particular. Three sights come to the fore: lying on top of a well filled with corpses, a woman, naked, covered in blood, one breast hacked off and stuffed in her mouth, her legs spread and a man's cut arm stuffed up her vagina; the steps of a temple, strewn with the cadavers and slippery with the battered brains of seven small children; in a doorway, a decapitated dog lying on the chest of a man who had been castrated.

Guarded by two smoke and sweat stained centurions, I found only one house full of the living – though they might have preferred it otherwise. Thirty or forty women were inside. Women? Many were not yet so. The sobs, the torn clothing, the straw mattresses in rows on the floor told me all I needed to know. One of the centurions interrupted my survey of this misery. 'Better be off, sir,' he said. 'There are two maniples due in any minute now.'

'Two?' I asked him. 'How many more will take their turn?'

'I don't know, sir,' he said. 'There's a rota published for the whole army. But at fifteen men a day, I doubt the women'll last too long. Three have died already. So we're taking the maniples *two at a time according to length of service, and giving each man three minutes—'*

*   'All right, centurion. Thank you,' I interrupted. 'I'll be on my way.' I had never encountered a rubric for rape before. But then this is Rome, after all.*

Note found on creased and dirty sheet of papyrus in the citadel of Carthage. It was unsigned, and the only example of this hand I found. But I am in no doubt as to the author: Fetopa, wife of Hanno

I have my period, and in this citadel there is nowhere to hide my bloody towels. I am ashamed. This man I married disappoints me. He has thought only for his memoir, and hopes only of rescue from the sea. My children fret and fight and are afraid. But I know what must be done. I—. [*Here the sheet was torn, and here we have Fetopa's only document – which is why I have told the scribes to include it. It is assumed that men determine, and record, events in which women are mere ciphers. I wonder when that will change?*]

A week of destruction later, sweat sprayed off the two hundred dripping soldiers as they heaved, and heaved, and heaved again. I had to cover my ears at the booming, crunching noise of splintering wood and buckling brass. The doors of Carthage's citadel seemed to sigh, but did not move. Then just as the Romans were swinging back the deadly ram again, its sharp point of iron, its timber dressed with lead, just then the vast doors sheathed with brass swung open, inward, of their own accord. Smoke billowed out. I felt the heat of a great fire burning within.

Scipio was in front of me, at his insistence and against his officers' advice there at the front for the final fall. The soldiers, in muttering agitation, were lowering the ram just as we passed. Scipio unsheathed his sword, hesitated, took off his helmet, put it and his sword down and then moved forward, climbing the penultimate set of steps to the open doors. He froze.

In a shift torn and filthy, his hair matted, his legs red and brown with blood, demented, the man who came to meet him was known to me. I knew also who the woman had to be. They stood on the citadel's threshold above Scipio, the man swaying, panting. The woman stood still beside him, her dress of purple clean and new, a woman with a mass of lustrous chestnut hair and a scar across one cheek. She seemed composed and calm. Perhaps, I thought, she is drugged. Or perhaps she knows the opiates of the mind that suffering brings.

Scipio took one step forwards. Hanno shook his head and screamed: 'Rome, I curse you!' He held out a dagger to the sinking sun. As Scipio rushed forward, Hanno slit his throat, left to right. Falling first to his knees, rich red bubbling from his mouth he slumped, blood spraying, cadaver convulsing.

Fetopa did not move. She stared at us and looked down at her dying husband. I may be wrong, but I would say she sneered. Then she raised her head, flicked back her hair, turned and darted back into the citadel, moving like a dancer, light upon her toes. Scipio stepped forwards. He grappled with and picked up Hanno, flailing in his death throes, and, grunting, slung him over his shoulder. I saw Hanno's blood pump wet down Scipio's back and legs, oozing everywhere. I heard Scipio cry out to Jupiter. I saw his tears.

Following, picking my way carefully up the bloody steps, even through the swelling smoke I smelled the cloying sweetness. I heard the sawing buzz of many thousand flies, feasting on putrescence. I too entered the citadel. I saw the very many, throats all cut, lying in their brown and spreading blood.

That room gave way to a wide outside terrace, an extended battlement high above where the temple of Eschmoun had been. Ferocious, there the pyre burned. There Scipio and I saw Fetopa, three hundred paces away, take a rough wooden ladder from the wall and throw it against the raging pyre. Then she climbed, her hair and clothes first singeing, then flaring to the flame. She did not scream. We stood transfixed as she moved upwards, step by step, through the licking blaze, the roaring fire. Just for a moment, she stood, a human torch, at the top. She faced us, her arms spread wide. In defiance, one historian would say, in supplication another; valediction, a third. For me, I do not know. But I have known war for thirty years. I have seen men die defiant, delirious, mad, or defecating at the dark. I have never seen such courage.

Scipio was on his knees, weeping silent tears. Wide-eyed, the bloody torso of Hanno was on its back before him. They say that blood is red. It is many colours. But I had, like Scipio, to watch. Holding a fold of my cloak across my face against the pyre's heat, I moved forward beyond Scipio. I stepped over Hanno. I am, after all, an historian. 'Historia' means 'enquiry' in Greek. I do not know what that is in Punic. I will find some Carthaginians in Corinth and ask them – if there are any there or, if so, any spared.

Fetopa's hair was burned now. Her flesh was gone, her ribs and thighs and knees and shins were white against the red, against the black, and still the fire rose up against the death of mutilated Carthage. I saw the skin on Fetopa's face becoming incandescent, blister, bubble and drop down like blobs of wax. Her lower lip fell off intact and sizzled on fierce faggots. I saw her cheekbones, her jaw, her skull appear, and still she stood, a living skeleton *in sepulchre. When does life end? Where does it go? What, to such a death, are the postulates of philosophy? The arms of what had been Fetopa dropped down. Smoke enshrouded her. With a sparkling, crackling crash, she fell. All was smell, the stench of charring flesh, and seasoned flames as when you roast a mallard over cherry wood, or over oak spit beef.*

A sharp sound to my right caught my attention. Cutting through the pyre's compelling cacophony, I heard the screech of a chair's legs on floor. On the far side of that necropolis, there, by a window, I saw a man, sitting, looking out to sea. He turned towards us. Again, I knew who it had to be. He of Chalcedon, Bostar.

Over the weeks that followed, I tried many times to speak to him in his tent pitched, on Scipio's express orders, next to ours. Silent, he simply stared, sometimes chewing his beloved bdellium. *Until, one evening when the rain was lashing and the wind came sheer from the sea, I looked in on him as usual. He was utterly impassive. I was turning to leave. 'You are Polybius,' he said suddenly: a statement, not a question.*

'I am,' I replied.

'I have three favours to ask of you,' he went on, staring through me, past me, to some place beyond my head.

'And they are?'

'One, for a stylus and parchment, or a wax tablet, if you prefer.'

'Of course. And the second?'

'That you have what I write delivered, if you can.'

'I will try,' I said. 'The third?'

For the first and last time he looked at me, into me. I sensed a soul racked with pain. 'Tell Scipio,' he faltered, and cleared his throat. 'Ask Scipio to—. Ask Scipio to forgive me. Tell him the answer is at the lake, on the island where we buried his father, where the water laps and herons raise their young. He should go there. He will understand, if he tries.' With that, Bostar closed his eyes and, through his nose, inhaled.

'Bostar, may I ask you one thing?' I said, pulling the tent's flap back against the wind and rain.

'Yes,' he replied. 'What is it?'

'You sit here, day after day, and move only to go to the latrines. What do you do?'

His eyes opened, and he smiled. He blinked once, twice, and closed his eyes. 'I think, Polybius,' he said very slowly, 'of synonyms for the adjective "naïve".'

As it happens, we had no tablets left, nor parchment. Other matters concern the quartermasters of a sack and siege. The notes I was making were in my mind. So I gave Bostar the Carthaginian equivalent, a dried leaf of the talipot palm. I had found a box of them amid the wreckage. Bound together, the Carthaginians make them into books, like wide rulers drilled and strung together. They call them ola books. I have several in my library here. Some are very beautiful, their ends of ivory inlaid with gold. Theirs is a craft the world will see no more.

So Bostar wrote his message on a talipot and gave it to me. But all our couriers were away. So I kept Bostar's palm. In the light of what happened, it did not seem appropriate to pass it to a courier, even when we got to Rome. I still have it here, and now we are about to leave for Corinth I will give it to a courier – for all the good that will do. The talipot says, in perfect Latin: 'Bostar of Chalcedon, to Trimalchio, master of the Apollodorus at Ostia, or at home in Liguria. I am where you left me. Come for me.' That is all.

Bostar never spoke to me again, nor answered my questions. Then one day, he wasn't there. No one had seen him leave. I asked Scipio to order a search for him. He laughed, and shook his head. In a world of many mysteries, the disappearance of Bostar troubles my mind.

But that was later. Having seen to the burial of the bloated bodies from the citadel, Scipio supervised the beginning of the destruction of what remained of Carthage, stone by bitter stone. Astylax the Carthaginian played a pivotal role. Scipio was an automaton. He washed and scrubbed himself when he was not working. 'Blood, blood, blood,' in his dreams he muttered from *the tent that we still shared. He complained of constipation. I recommended the juice of prunes, but he preferred to suffer. I only wished that he would do so in silence. Dust filled our every orifice. Smoke stung our smarting eyes. Its smell filled our clothes, our beds, our souls. The city's baths were broken up. We stank. We itched. We grew fallow in our own reek.*

One night I awoke, troubled, sweating, sure that something was wrong. By the light of the lamp that Scipio insisted was kept burning, I could see that his billet was empty. I got up, put on my sandals and wrapped a cloak about me. Our tent flap was untied. The guard outside snapped to attention. 'Where is Scipio?' I asked him.

'I don't know, sir,' he replied. 'He went that way,' the soldier said pointing, 'to the city.'

'Or to what's left of it,' I mumbled, rubbing my eyes.

'What's that, sir?'

'Nothing, soldier, nothing. As you were.' I walked off towards the smoking, smouldering remains of Carthage.

I found Scipio, eventually. He was standing on the pile of stones that marked where the temple of Eschmoun had been. Through scudding clouds a half moon lit the melancholy scene. If he saw me or heard me, Scipio gave no sign. He was muttering to himself. I could not hear.

'What are you saying, Scipio?' I called out, as gently as I could. His eyes turned to me. He saw me, as if for the first time. He raised his voice, and I caught the rhythm of Homer's hexameters, repeated again and again:

ἔσσεται ἦμαρ ὅτ’ ἄν ποτ’ ὀλώλῃ Ἴλιος ἱρὴ
καὶ Πρίαμος καὶ λαὸς ἐϋμμελίω Πριάμοιο.

A day will come when Ilium, that holy city, will perish
And Priam also will perish, and his people, skilled in handling
the spear.

I listened to the elegy of Scipio for Carthage. I thought of Aristotle, and how if first we fear for Carthage, then we fear for ourselves. But Rome still stood, and Scipio was born to serve her. I rubbed my face and scratched my beard. 'Come, Scipio, come,' I said, interrupting his recital. 'Bed, and then Corinth, call.'

Three days later, Scipio handed command to a young proconsul, Gaius Calpurnius Piso. I regard it as a fitting irony that, when he began his career, Piso was a client of Cato's patronage. He had arrived with three more legions and a further thousand pioneers, his orders to leave nothing but the wind. The augurs and priests of Rome had come as well with their rituals, their extispicy and imprecations – and a plough. They were to cut one furrow round where the walls of Carthage had stood, and cast salt into it, so that nothing would ever grow again, and curse the site to execration in the memory of man. Carthage was to be barren, void, perished as though it had never been, mute memorial to the plenipotence of Rome.

I have it on good authority, being as I have said an historian, that this is now so.

The evening Scipio and I left Carthage, the two of us, alone, before we went back to Rome and then on to another siege, another city, the sky was sullen. No stars shone. Past what must have been the great seaward wall of even Dido's city, from our cart we walked the last two hundred paces to our galley waiting in the inner, naval harbour, like the outer soon to be destroyed. From the middle of the rubble, I heard an infant's cry, a mewling in the stones. I checked, and cupped an ear. The sound had gone. Perhaps it was the wind, or some sleight of my mind. I walked on, and we cast off, away, out into nascent night.

To seek in unmixed wine a black and fatherless oblivion, Scipio went below. I stayed on deck, savouring the first clean air that I had known for weeks, craning my neck to the breeze, feeling the lice scuttle in my beard. Halfway across the bay, the captain swore loudly. I took a step across the creaking deck towards him. 'What's wrong?' I asked.

'Damn! That'll slow us till we're round the point,' he muttered, shoving the rudder hard away and bringing the galley, sharply and shuddering, about. 'Plumblines and watch, on deck!' he roared, swinging his head down into the mouth of the hold. Turning to me, 'Look,' he whispered.

My eyes followed his pointing arm. I looked at the mass of Jebel-bou-Kournine, Carthage's sacred mountain. I could just make out its double horns against the lighter dark. In Rome, I thought, they will be lighting festive fires. But the light of Carthage burned no more.

Epilogue

I am Niarchos, an Athenian, but a clerk to Polybius here in Rome. My master has gone to Corinth, leaving us, as he has said, to bind these tesserae together. But before we transcribe them onto one roll – I think one will do, for this is not a long work – I will add these two more letters. They come from the pile of papers Polybius had gathered together, but has not read. Now, I suppose, he never will. When he returns, his mind will be on the last siege, the next sack. And anyway, his History awaits.

Letter found in the archives of Rome

Quintus Fulvius, harbourmaster at Ostia, to the quartermaster of the fleet, Titus Quinctius, in Rome. The transports have all arrived from the sack of Carthage, and disembarked their cargoes. The sale into slavery of those Carthaginians they carried will begin tomorrow and last for six days. But, as you know, 70,000 Poeni were to be brought. That is why you ordered, and I released, 200 transport ships to bring them here. Well, I have just completed the log. Only 173 transports are moored here in the harbour. Where are the missing 27, and the cargo they carried?

Letter found in the archives of Rome

Titus Quinctius to Quintus Fulvius. You are quite right that 27 transports have not returned from Carthage. I congratulate you on your acuity and diligence. It cannot have been easy to identify so small a discrepancy. Acting under orders, duly sealed and notarised and now lodged in the archives of the Senate, the ships in question were loaded with the Carthaginian wounded, sick, deformed and ill – some 9,000 of the survivors of the siege and sack. Their holds were battened down, their crews were taken off, and these said ships were sunk at sea. But I took great pains to ensure we used the oldest vessels only, those that were leaking, in need of caulking or well wormed. So do not distress yourself about the cost. Look forward, instead, to your share of the proceeds of the sale. Pray to Jupiter for sound teeth, and high prices. Ten times over will the Republic's share replace the value of some rotting hulks. We will replace the transports if need be. Or are there no more Carthages left for us to burn?

Chronology & Apology

149 BC	Death of Cato the Censor
	Third Punic War
148	Fourth Macedonian War
146	Carthage destroyed
	Corinth destroyed
	Macedonia becomes a Roman province
	Roman republic at its zenith
129	Death of Publius Cornelius Scipio Aemilianus Africanus (by then also Numantinus, an honorific for his conquest of Numantia)
118	Death of Polybius

This is the factual chronology. That of this novel differs in several ways. My main liberty has been to move back in time the third and final Punic War. I have done so in order that this fiction's principal protagonists of the war can be the bastard sons of those who led the second: Hannibal and Scipio Africanus. But it was in fact Scipio's adopted grandson, Publius Cornelius Scipio Aemilianus (Africanus minor) Numantinus, who commanded the Roman army in the final war. One Hasdrubal led the Carthaginians, and we know little of him but his name. All lesser anachronisms are of course deliberate – a word like 'gunnel' is a particular tease, but one I hope the late Patrick O'Brian would have enjoyed. 'Howdah' and 'mahout' I replaced and then, on the grounds of their semitic etymology, restored. If the Norse 'berserk' is an epoch too far, read the Indian *musth* if you prefer.

Among other things, my numismatics are suspect at best, and my treatment of illegitimacy is almost certainly baloney. The Romans knew a bastard as either *nothus*, born out of wedlock but to a known father, or *spurius*, born out of wedlock to an unknown father. There is no evidence that either could inherit under Roman law. So whether or not Scipio Africanus had a bastard son, it is most unlikely that the child could have become his heir. Because we have no evidence whatsoever, Hanno's succession is less contrived.

I have taken other liberties with history, but no more I believe than novelists are commonly allowed.

Anyway, why write a novel about Carthage, and try to conclude a trilogy of books about some far off and long forgotten wars? Because in the struggle to defeat Carthage, Rome found herself. Even now, that legacy still informs the best, and the worst, of what we are. We enhance our present and our future if we understand our past. Secondly, I hope in this novel to have explored the ambiguity of motive in people, politics and power. Yes, our world has changed since the second century BC. But the ambivalence that begets most actions stays the same.

As for sources, Polybius was an eyewitness to the final phase of the Third Punic War. But only fragments of his account survive: *Histories* XXXVII, 1&3; XXXVIII, 1–3 and XXXIX, 3–5 are germane. Appian drew heavily on then extant Polybius, and his *Roman History* VIII, 10–20.135 is the best ancient source. There are a few telling passages in Livy – e.g. XXXII, 2; XXXIII, 6–49 and XXXIV, 49, 62. Plutarch's *Cato* is useful as well, and his *Demetrius* is instructive about ancient siegecraft. The modern bibliography is of course learned – and long. Of the few contemporary Tunisian scholars, ancient Carthage and all who sailed in her have a rare and admirable advocate in M'hamed Hassine Fantar.

I thank my friend Gregory Wilsdon, whose enduring exactitude saved me from several errors. Despite him, I have on occasion confused *cognomina* with *praenomina*. Thanks to him, at last I know the difference.

Finally, for the third time but not, I hope, the last, I record my gratitude to my now octogenarian editor, Peter Cochrane. *Senex sapiens, gentilis vir.*

Ross Leckie
Edinburgh
April 2000